Love Bug

H.E. Goodhue

LOVE BUG

A tinny announcement played through the public address system, its large speakers looming high on every street corner. Cameras, much smaller and hardly noticeable, hung just below each speaker.

"It is the duty of every citizen to ensure that they have a functioning Em-Pak. It is the privilege and honor of every citizen to report those who do not. To remove one's Em-Pak is to choose death. The Emotions Regulatory Commission will not tolerate such traitorous behavior. All citizens must adhere to the Citizens' Safety Protocol. The virus cannot be allowed within the walls of your city. The Reds cannot be allowed to return. Emotions are weakness, flaws that lead to only one end. It is the duty of every citizen to ensure that they have a functioning Em-Pak."

This announcement played throughout the city every fifteen minutes, echoing through silent streets and off the sides of buildings. It was recited from memory at the beginning and end of each school day, a mantra, almost an incantation that kept the citizens safe. This was their pledge. This was the cost of safety.

Row upon row of gray buildings shone beneath a brilliantly blue sky like stones set in a riverbed. Few noticed the natural beauty of the sky, focused more on where they needed to be and what they needed to do. This cityscape would have once inspired man to splash paint across a canvas or to articulate those unsaid lines of poetry that resonated upon the strings of his heart. Once, this sky would have roused feelings of joy and happiness, made people late, if for no reason beyond getting lost in the beautiful expanse of its infinite dimensions. At one point, these sights would have been appreciated, these feelings cherished, but no more. Things such as beauty, art and music, no longer held value, having been outlawed and now ignored. These things were viewed as dangerous, as wastes of time that served no purpose beyond bringing citizens one-step closer to infection.

Fifty years had passed since the last citizen admired a painting or became lost in the picturesque notes of a musical composition. Fifty years, half a lifetime, was all it took for these things, once esteemed and treasured, to become erased, and simply cast aside. However, much can happen in fifty years, especially when each of those fifty is soaked with blood and tears. Citizens were willing to trade these once beloved objects for a sense of safety. They were willing to trade anything to be safe from the Reds.

Cars and transports glided past, making little noise beyond the gentle rumble of their engines. No one shouted, honked a horn or revved an engine impatiently, as if demanding a light to change faster. The sounds of traffic, now a thing of the past, had become obsolete with the institution of mandatory driving systems. History had taught that citizens could not be trusted to operate vehicles in a fashion that the Emotions Regulatory Commission found suitable. Perfectly sane people had fallen victim to the insanity that festered and coursed through the twisted asphalt veins that fed traffic jams. In the early days, before the virus was understood, this unbridled display of emotion, once known as a road rage, had led to massive outbreaks of Reds, costing hundreds of citizens their lives. Independent travel was simply too stressful, too unpredictable and therefore had been turned over to machines, acting in synchronized harmony to eliminate the dangers once posed by travel.

A need to control situations and perhaps more importantly, emotions had led to the advent of a new technological age. The ERC simply could not allow emotions to run rampant, creating fertile ground for a new crop of Reds. Emotions, these intense character flaws, once celebrated, now needed to be blunted, controlled. Em-Paks appeared to be a Godsend, an almost vaccination against the virus and guarantee that one would never become a Red.

These small, oblong boxes, no bigger than a house key, were now implanted at the base of each citizen's neck at birth. Only a small section of the Em-Paks remained visible after they were in place. Few citizens ever saw a one before implantation and none cared to after. Too much knowledge was dangerous thing, so the ERC sought to control it. Still, hushed whispers spoke of

2

mechanical spiders and tiny machines buried in the neck of each citizen.

Em-Paks became part of each citizen, providing a means through which his or her emotions could be blunted. Ensuring emotional stability was the cornerstone of the ERC's Citizens' Safety Protocol. There could be no choice with Em-Paks. The safety of all citizens depended upon it. Laws and severe punishments for failing to adhere to them had to be enacted. Removal of one's Em-Pak put all other citizens at risk.

All these sacrifices were made in the name of survival and to ensure that the human race could survive the virus, survive the violence of the Reds. There was no other choice.

-2-

"Cora Eldritch?" the instructor asked, a hint of irritation in his voice. A soft beep from the instructor's Em-Pak and all signs of frustration melted from his face. "Cora, are you with us?"

Cora was lost in her thoughts and had forgotten that today was a special day, a day she, above all people, should have remembered.

"Oh? Um, yes?" Cora mumbled, trying to will her attention off the two squirrels outside and back into the classroom. Her Em-Pak let out a small chirp, correcting the feelings of embarrassment that flared up and they disappeared. "Yes, Mr. Thomas."

"Very good," Mr. Thomas nodded, "now would you like to tell the class what is special about today?"

Cora knew that there was no surprise for her to reveal. All the students knew what was special about the day, every citizen did. But this routine was her birthright and something she was expected to perform every year. Clearing her throat, Cora tried to find some way to care about a story she had told enough times to know that she couldn't have cared less.

"Em-Paks were created today," Cora said flatly. The students around her looked on with blank expressions. This story was something they had heard every year as well and they probably could have told just as well as Cora.

"Yes," Mr. Thomas agreed, "and who do we credit with the invention that now keeps all of us from becoming infected?"

"Samuel Eldritch...my grandfather," Cora muttered. The Reds killed him before Cora was born, but she had still lived every day of her life in his shadow.

"Samuel Eldritch is who we remember today," Mr. Thomas said, pausing to look each student in the face. The students nodded uncomfortably, hoping that would be enough to make their teacher move on to the next. "Samuel Eldritch, inventor of the Em-Pak and savior of the human race. No doubt, he's left you some very large shoes to fill, Cora, but an honor nonetheless. Wouldn't you say?"

"Yes, Mr. Thomas, an honor," Cora replied, but her voice held no conviction. "He, uh, was a great man."

"Absolutely," Mr. Thomas agreed. "Today, we remember the gift that Samuel Eldritch's invention bestowed upon us. We were adrift in a sea of chaos and blood, battling friends and family who had fallen ill. The Em-Pak is what separates us from them. It is what keeps our emotions in check. It keeps us human." Mr. Thomas paused. "Remember students that anyone, anyone who is infected is dangerous. Once a person changes, they are no long your mother or best friend, they are a Red and they must be reported and sanitized." The students nodded. This was a lesson they had been taught since they were little. Being sixteen, it was now ingrained in their person.

"Mr. Thomas?" Richie Abrams raised his hand. Richie was smaller than many of the other boys and prone to asking endless strings of questions. Cora had always found him to be okay, which was really the most that could be said about anything.

There had always been quiet whispers between students, nothing more than rumors really, but talk nonetheless about how emotions felt. Cora and her peers were the first generation to have had Em-Paks since birth, never having felt anything beyond 'okay' and having no real knowledge of emotions.

"Yes, Richie?" Mr. Thomas groaned, the Em-Pak correcting his feelings of annoyance.

"Where is Abby?" Richie asked, showing as much concern as was allowed by his Em-Pak.

"Abby?" Mr. Thomas repeated, as if he had already forgotten the missing student. "Her father was found to be unsuitable." The students knew what this meant. "He had a malfunctioning Em-Pak and his family failed to report him. We all know that the Citizens' Safety Protocol demands that she should have turned him in to the nearest ERC office."

"She didn't?" Richie persisted.

"No," Mr. Thomas replied, his tone serious and dark. "Her father disabled his family's Em-Paks. Fortunately, a neighbor noticed them acting strangely and reported it. ERC officers collected the entire family. They all conspired to commit emotional treason."

"But why would someone do that?" Richie continued. "Wouldn't that put them at risk for infection?"

"Yes, it would," Mr. Thomas answered. "But I can't even pretend to know why someone would do that. It is possible that some misguided affection for his family could lead him to do so, but I fail to see how turning into a Red would benefit one's family. And that, children, is why we need to remember how very lucky we are today. We have been gifted with the invention of the Em-Pak and that is what separates us from those beasts."

"Are they really beasts?" Richie cut in. "Like animals?" Cora could hear the other students' Em-Paks beeping, a chorus of tinny chimes. They were all growing tired of Richie's persistent questions, but by the time the lunch bell tolled, all would be forgotten. With blunted emotions, arbitrary social constructs like popularity and bullying had never entered Cora's classroom, their toxic seeds never finding fertile soil for their twisted roots.

"No, Richie," Mr. Thomas responded. "The Reds aren't actually beasts, at least not in the story book sense you're thinking of. As we have discussed before, the Reds were once like us, but without Em-Paks, they contracted the virus. Once infected, the Reds became violent and overwhelmed by their anger. Any emotion is a gateway to infection, which is why Abby is no longer a member of this class. Her family's citizenship has been forfeited."

It was that simple. Abby was gone, as was the rest of her family. She had committed no crime beyond being her father's daughter, but that was enough. Anyone at risk of becoming a Red simply vanished. The students in Cora's class had heard this lesson many times before. Reds were dangerous, were deadly and needed to be eradicated.

"But why are there still Reds?" Richie carried on. "Why hasn't the ERC wiped them out?"

Mr. Thomas's Em-Pak began working overtime. "Richie, we mustn't question the ERC."

"No, no," Richie added quickly. "I...I...I just..."

"Richie just meant how could the Reds still be around when the ERC is working so hard to protect us. The Reds are just mindless monsters, so it's hard to believe that they can hide from the ERC," Cora said, coming to the boy's rescue. "Right?"

"Yeah, yes," Richie nodded enthusiastically, "that's what I meant."

"Of course," Mr. Thomas agreed. "Thank you, Cora, for clarifying."

"You're welcome," Cora waved. Cora's face was a mask of indifference even though her Em-Pak remained silent. She had been trained from birth to handle situations like this, to reroute people's thinking and get them to see the value in absolute subservience to the ERC.

"Some Em-Paks malfunction from accidents," Mr. Thomas answered. "Those poor unfortunate souls still must be removed. Then there are the traitorous Emos, those people ignorant enough to try to live without an Em-Pak. Their settlements are what keep the ERC from completely wiping out the Red threat."

Cora listened as a few of the students' Em-Paks chirped, smoothing the edges of rough feelings. Her own device added to the chorus.

"Yes, yes," Mr. Thomas nodded, noting the students' reactions. "Upsetting for sure. Very upsetting indeed that your classmate failed us all and committed emotional treason. And talk of the Reds as well, upsetting indeed."

Cora could briefly feel something, some strange unpleasantness that disappeared before she could name it. That must have been what her teacher meant by 'upset', Cora thought, but she pushed it out of her mind.

"Now back to things of actual importance," Mr. Thomas continued. "In a few moments, we'll be switching on our viewing monitors to see Assemblyman Eldritch deliver a speech from the capital, commemorating his father's, Cora's grandfather's, tremendous accomplishment. Quite a day for your family, Ms. Eldritch."

Eyes settled on Cora once again. She could feel the small prickle on heat on the back of her neck, but lacked the words to express why. They were all waiting for her to say something. That was her birthright, her duty.

"Yes, thank you, Mr. Thomas," Cora answered. "Both great men. A great day for all of us, really." Cora waited, judging her teacher and classmates' reactions. Had she said what they expected? Had she performed her role? The small waves of heat began to dance on the back of her neck again.

"Indeed," Mr. Thomas smiled faintly. He then turned to switch on the large monitor in the front of the classroom.

Cora stared blankly at the image of her father. It was the most she had seen of him in days, and later, she would have to pretend to know him in front of countless cameras and viewers. Her Em-Pak chirped loudly as she thought of another dreadful limo ride with her mother and spoiled brother; another day for her to dance for the masses, all for the sake of her father's political career and to lay to groundwork for her own. All these decisions, of which Cora had no say, but that mandated the direction of her life, weighed down upon her, pressing her head closer and closer to the desk.

"Cora?" Mr. Thomas asked, a hint of worry coloring his words momentarily. "Are you alright?"

The Em-Pak securely implanted at the base of Cora's neck beeped once again. All of those prior thoughts, independent and dangerous, vanished with the faint ping of three mechanical notes.

Cora would once again wave and smile because that was what was expected of her. That was her role to play, no matter how badly some small piece of her wanted otherwise.

As Assemblyman Eldritch took the stage, Cora's Em-Pak chirped once again.

-3-

The grass was cool with early morning dew that tickled bare feet and wet the rolled up legs of Remmy's pants. This was the best time to be out in the fields, when no one else was there to shatter the silence. Remmy would wake early every morning and slip out of his family's tent so that he could steal a few precious moments alone in the field. This habit worried his mother, made her entertain visions of Reds tearing her only child apart. The truth of the matter was that Remmy knew the dangers of being alone and still felt it was worth the risk. Besides, it had been weeks since anyone had even seen a Red, let alone been attacked by one. It was far more likely that an ERC patrol would pick him up, but even that, couldn't keep Remmy safely in his cot. Those fleeting moments of early morning where the birds began to sing and colors streaked the sky, colors that seemed to exist nowhere else, was Remmy's world. That was what he lived for.

A separate world existed that Remmy barely understood. A world of Em-Paks and the ERC, where people had given up their ability to feel emotions because they were convinced that it kept them safe from the Reds and the Love Bug. Remmy knew there was a real name for the virus, something scientific and probably full of hyphenated numbers and letters, but he preferred the slang name. Love Bug just seemed to fit, besides that was what most of the Emos called it.

That name, Emos, Remmy hated, but that was what they were, at least to the ERC and all of those people behinds the walls of the cities. The first people to discover the method and means of removing their Em-Paks had been called 'Emotionals' because the ERC wanted to discredit what these rebels were after and brand them guilty of emotional treason. Regardless of what they were called, they were only one thing to the ERC, criminals. Even this idea was strange to Remmy. He had been born outside the city walls and had never been fitted with an Em-Pak. Many of the older members and new arrivals had the telltale rows of scars on the back of their necks where an Em-Pak had once sat, but not Remmy.

Remmy's parents told him that they had escaped when his mother became pregnant. The pregnancy had been unsanctioned by the ERC, but his parents refused to give Remmy up. His mother told him it was because they knew he was special, destined for great things. Remmy liked this explanation, but knew the truth was that his parents loved him, loved him so much that even their Em-Paks couldn't stifle it. That had been reason enough to defy the ERC.

Most of the time, life was simple for Remmy. School, chores and then time in the fields was what Remmy expected from each day. The routine of it was boring, but on days where they would have to collapse tents, leave behind belongings and throw anything within arm's reach into the backs of the vehicles, Remmy knew how lucky he truly was. These were days that ERC patrols were getting too close, days where Remmy's routine could be permanently destroyed. Somehow, everyone in Remmy's camp managed to stay one-step ahead of the ERC and would set up in another spot and start living again.

No one really knew what the ERC would do if they captured any Emos. Some thought that they would be refitted with Em-Paks, but this was only rumors and fear. The truth was that once someone had removed their Em-Pak, the scars made it impossible to implant the device again. Maybe in the early days, the ERC had tried to put the Em-Paks back, but Remmy suspected that they wouldn't waste the time these days. No, ERC patrols were not looking to bring people back. They were far more interested in eliminating possible future Reds and punishing those guilty of emotional treason.

Remmy, as a young boy, had struggled to understand all these titles, these words that seemed no worse than others did, but that seemed to signify massive differences between himself and other people. His parents had done their best to explain to Remmy that the word 'Reds' was an old one from the early days of the virus. The virus had overwhelmed people's emotions, making them violent and irrational and left them as little more than screaming, rage filled shells of their former selves. Around the uninfected, Reds would scream uncontrollably, while trying to tear them apart.

The color of their faces, as well as the blood they left behind, resulted in them becoming known as Reds.

"But why?" Remmy would ask. "How can emotions be bad?"

His parents would smile, satisfied with their decision to defy the ERC. "Emotions aren't bad, Remmy," his mother would smile. "Anger is bad. Rage is bad. People used to think that all emotions were dangerous, even love. That's why the ERC makes people wear Em-Paks, but then, they can't feel anything."

"Even love? They think love is bad?" Young Remmy would question.

"Yes, the people living behind the city walls, think even love is dangerous," Remmy's mother would continue, "but we know different. All the Emos do and that's why we escaped from the cities and removed our Em-Paks before we forgot what love felt like."

"Doesn't that mean we can get sick too?" Remmy's eyes would go wide with fear.

His mother would smile and pull him close. "Don't worry, Rem. There is still danger from the Love Bug, but if we remember to keep our anger from getting the better of us, then we're safe."

"But what about the Reds?" Remmy would persist, knowing this conversation would delay his bedtime.

"Well, sweetie," his mother would sigh, "the Reds are still very dangerous, but we can avoid them."

"But what *are they?*" Remmy would almost whisper.

"They were once like us, but not anymore. Not once they became ill," his mother answered honestly.

"*Where are they?*" Remmy would gasp.

"No one has ever seen," his mother would reply. "The Reds are hidden away somewhere and only come out to hunt."

"They're wild," Remmy would add, "like animals."

"No," his mother would interject, a serious look on her face. "Never think of the Reds like that. They are dangerous and capable of far more than any animal. They travel in small groups and set traps. The ERC wants people to think the Reds are little more than wild animals, but we have learned so much after leaving the cities, Remmy. The Reds can think and plan. You must never underestimate them."

Remmy had nightmares about the Reds for much of his early years. His young mind pieced together his parent's stories to create the terrifying image of red faced, screaming demons that could rise up out of nowhere, snatch him away and eat him. But as Remmy grew older and encountered Reds a few times, he saw that they could be avoided.

Now at the age of sixteen, Remmy had learned to pick his way through the fields carefully, listening for the telltale rumble of a Red's throat. Hearing this noise, Remmy would drop to the ground or scramble into a nearby tree to wait for the Red to wander past, but there was still a very real reason to fear the Reds.

The morning Remmy awoke to see the Martinez's tent in tatters was carved into his memory, each line jagged and painful. They had been there only hours before, the entire Martinez family, but all that was left in the morning was a tangled mess of canvas and blood. At first, everyone thought that one of the Martinez family members must have turned and that the Martinez's missing daughter, Jessica, must have caught the Love Bug, killed her family and run off.

Remmy's young mind struggled to comprehend how you share dinner with someone, share minutes of your life with them, only to awaken a few hours later and find them torn apart, dead. Was that really how life worked? Could it be that simple? Remmy's mother had told him that it was and that you never knew when someone's life could end, so you needed to cherish every moment. This idea brought Remmy no comfort.

The following night, the Red came back. It was one lone child, no older than nine or ten. It wasn't Jessica. Being alone and so small, it was easy for him to slip past the watch and into the Martinez's tent. But could one small boy really kill an entire family? Remmy had a hard time believing so, but watching how it took five full-grown men to finally subdue and silence him, left no doubt. Silence him was how Remmy's mother had explained it to him. That was the only way he could wrap his mind around what he witnessed. At the time, that Red hadn't been much older than Remmy - it could have been Remmy.

"What happened to Jessica?" Remmy demanded, his thin shoulders heaving up and down, tiny fists balled tight with anger.

"She's gone," his father answered simply.

"Where?" Remmy snapped. "We need to find her."

"Rem," his father said as he knelt down to look at his son, "no one comes back from where the Reds take them. I know Jessica was your friend, but she's gone, buddy. I'm sorry."

"I wish I had killed him," Remmy growled, shocking his parents.

"No," Remmy's mother almost cried. "No you don't. Don't say that."

"Why?" Remmy cried. "Why not? Jessica was my friend!"

"Which is why the others silenced that Red for you, Rem," his father answered calmly. "We should never kill a Red that killed one of our own. It's too easy for rage to take hold. What you will do is help bury the Red in the morning."

"Bury him?" Remmy spat. "Why would I do that?"

"Because you can't bury Jessica," his father replied. "It's how you will learn to let go of your anger. We must forgive the Reds because what they do isn't their fault. They're sick, so there's no reason for us to be angry with the Reds. We can be sad, but never be angry."

Remmy tried to accept his father's explanation, tried to believe it. All of the other Emos appeared to live by this rule. In the morning, Remmy buried the Red that killed his friend, shoveling both his anger and dirt into the hole.

That had happened years ago, somehow becoming understood or at least accepted, but never forgotten. Never knowing what happened to Jessica was something that Remmy simply couldn't explain away.

Remmy quietly moved through the tall grass, pausing when the brush to his left rustled and then breathing a sigh of relief when a large buck bounded out. Things made sense out here, seemed to follow an easily understood order, not like school.

Going to classes had never been something that Remmy enjoyed, but there really was no choice. From a young age, all Emos were taught to control their emotions through meditation and breathing, learning never to become too angry. Remmy found these periods of time to be excruciating. Why spend time inhaling and exhaling, counting seconds in between and focusing on images in your mind? Sure that kept the Emo children calm, kept them safe from the Love Bug, but it also took away from the time they could be enjoying the world. Remmy focused enough in his classes to make his parents happy and to keep him out of trouble with the teacher, but those lessons were never what calmed him. It was these moments, alone in the fields and surrounded by nature, which kept Remmy from becoming a Red. The thought of never being able to enjoy another sunrise was more than enough to keep Remmy's emotions in check.

The buck leapt effortlessly through the high grass, appearing almost to hang frozen in the air for a few seconds before dropping back into the tangled mass below. Remmy became transfixed by the ease with which the animal moved and found himself stumbling after it.

With one forceful leap, the buck launched itself from the thick underbrush and into the street. Its hooves clicked loudly on the blacktop, sounding oddly discordant and hollow against the high-pitched melody of the bird's songs. Remmy typically avoided the streets, fearing ERC patrols, but the deer seemed to wait for him, almost beckoning him to follow.

One tentative step onto the macadam and then another, Remmy's hand trembled as he reached out to try to touch the deer. Its antlers spread from each side, easily capable of harming Remmy, but there was no threat. Remmy's fingers gently brushed the hindquarter of the buck moments before the throaty roar of a Red and then another and another filled the air.

The buck, sensing danger, sprang forward and dashed into the woods. Remmy turned to see a writhing mass of Reds heading towards him. He had never seen more than two or three together, but now, they were so closely packed together that counting them became impossible.

Remmy turned to run. A strange object hurtled towards him from the other direction. A long sleek black vehicle unlike anything Remmy had ever seen careened towards him. Another mass of Reds could be seen sprinting behind it, their screams drowning out the mechanical protests of the engine as the driver pushed the vehicle to go faster.

Turning back in the direction he had previously come, Remmy dove into the undergrowth and scrambled towards the nearest copse of trees. Thorns and dead branches ripped at his back and arms, but Remmy had no time to think about such minor injuries. He needed to avoid the Reds and to warn everyone in his camp, warn his parents.

A loud *crash* echoed through the field, followed by the groan of metal twisted to unnatural angles and the scattering of glass. Remmy's head bumped into the thick trunk of an old pine. Without looking back, he leapt into the branches and climbed higher and higher. Trees were not the perfect hiding place, but Remmy had never seen a Red try to climb one, let alone succeed.

The mangled remains of both the vehicle and the Reds were strewn about the field.

"Must have crashed into each other," Remmy panted as he steadied himself on a limb. At least the threat was gone. Whoever had been in that long, strange car wasn't so lucky, but Remmy tried not to think about them.

Then he heard her. A thin wail echoed from inside the twisted wreck. A girl's voice, desperate for help and raw with pain, cried out to anyone who could hear. Remmy hesitated. There was no way to know who this girl was or if she was ERC. As Remmy saw another tangled mass of Reds cresting the top of the nearest hill, heading directly towards the wreck, those concerns no longer mattered.

Before he knew what he was doing, Remmy had dropped from the safety of the old pine and was heading directly towards the crash.

-4-

The ride to the Stele had been pretty much, what Cora expected. Her brother lost in a video game, her mother ignoring them, looking up only to bark an order or two and Cora silently sitting in the limo, wishing she were anywhere else. She hated the Stele. It was the main city and filled with countless monuments to her grandfather. A large stone slab stood upright in the center of the Stele, giving the city its name. The image of Cora's grandfather was carved into the stone with an inscription commemorating the date he unveiled the Em-Pak and become an ERC saint. This was where Cora's father would stand to deliver his speech and where Cora would have to perform for the masses.

Cora knew that her Em-Pak dulled her emotions, so she could only imagine how excruciating a family road trip would have been without one. Moments like these were the fleeting few where Cora was actually glad to have the stupid thing. Otherwise, her thoughts would inevitably wander to contemplating what life would feel like without the Em-Pak. Cora knew that it would be a very short life, thanks to the Reds and virus, but still she couldn't help but wonder what it would be like to feel. Would things be different? Did the Emos that her father called terrorists and hated so profoundly really know something she didn't? Was the risk worth it?

The limo's soundproof cabin prevented Cora and her family from hearing the cries of the Reds as they closed in on the vehicle. Up front, their security officer pressed the correct buttons to override the guidance system. A machine wouldn't be able to evade these things. There was no rational pattern to Reds' behavior, so programming a guidance system to evade them was essentially impossible. All ERC vehicles with clearance to travel between cities were equipped with an override, allowing the security officers to take control, but never had it been used to avoid this many Reds.

The thick glass divider slid down, revealing the security officer's panicked look. "We've got a problem," he croaked. Seconds later, his Em-Pak chirped loudly and he appeared calm.

"Don't worry, Mrs. Eldritch, I'll get us through this." He pressed the button to once again raise the tinted divider, but not before Cora saw a massive knot of people bearing down on their car. They looked wild, screaming and waving crude weapons. Their faces were all set in the same feral expression of rage and washed in crimson hues. Reds.

"Mom?" Cora asked, a note of concern vanishing with a single mechanical beep.

"We'll be fine, sweetie," Mrs. Eldritch waved dismissively, using the term of endearment out of habit, not affection. "Just sit back and relax."

"Don't be stupid, Cora!" Xander snapped. "They're just animals. You'll probably have a full blown melt down if we pass a deer." Cora's brother, Xander, was twelve, but had already begun to prepare for his entrance into the politics. He idolized their father and resented the attention he felt was wasted on Cora. If an Eldritch was going to be the head of the ERC, Xander was determined it be him.

The world suddenly felt upended, the laws of gravity momentarily no longer keeping Cora and her family safely planted on the plush leather benches of the limo. A blinding flash of white pain shot through Cora's mind. Loud shrieks filled the cabin of the limo. Cora's mind struggled to place the sounds. Were the sounds from the crash? Was it the Reds?

As the limo finished its tumble through the field, Cora realized the sound had been coming from her own mouth. Her head throbbed and her throat was raw. An eerie silence settled over the passenger cabin of the limo. Dappled sunlight danced through the interior, filtered through cracked tinted windows.

"Mom?" Cora called again, the word calling to mind memories of her mother's dismissive response from moments before. "Xander? Are you okay?" Her brother groaned, but didn't respond. Cora's mother was silent. In the front of the limo, the security officer cursed loudly, sliding through shattered glass.

"Ms. Eldritch, stay here," the officer grunted as he slid out the broken side window. He drew his pistol and quickly scanned the area. "I'm sure that a recovery team is en route. Stay here where it's safe, there may be more-..." The officer's words were cut short as two sets of filthy hands clamped over his face and pulled him to the ground. A loud shriek followed by three erratic pistol shots filled the air outside of the ruined limo.

Something banged against the side of the limo. Blood, thick and red began to run down the side of the limo's door creating the image of a hellish waterfall. It pooled and began slowly to seep further into the vehicle.

Pain radiated through Cora's body, but another odd sensation filled her mind. Something twisted in Cora's insides, tightening around her heart and making it hard to breathe.

"Xander? Xander, please," Cora pleaded. A throaty scream resonated outside of the limo. More could be heard in the distance.

The strange feeling tangling itself around Cora's insides intensified. Bile burned the back of her throat. For the first time in her life, Cora felt fear.

Cora tried to stifle it, tried to keep her mouth closed, but with no practice, Cora was unable to keep the scream inside.

A voice in Remmy's head screamed for him to stop. What he was doing was completely stupid, he knew that it was, but he couldn't stop himself. Something about the girl's scream called to him, beckoned to some innate primal urge to protect.

Moments before Remmy dropped from the tree, he watched an ERC officer crawl out from the vehicle. The man drew a pistol and checked the surrounding area, but failed to look on the top of the wrecked limo. Two Reds descended on him, dragging him to the ground, tearing into the soft flesh of his face with hands and teeth. The ERC officer flailed, firing shots wildly. One found its target and dropped the Red to the ground.

The second Red lifted the ERC officer from the ground and slammed him against the side of the ruined vehicle. Screaming wildly, the Red buried its teeth in the man's throat. Blood gushed from the wound, coating the door of the vehicle.

Remmy had seen blood before, remembered the Martinez family, but he had never seen carnage of this sort, had never been front row to observe the Reds' violence firsthand. It was overwhelming, like stumbling into the middle of someone else's nightmare.

The girl screamed again and the Red's attention was suddenly drawn inside the wreck. More Reds stampeded towards Remmy and the crash site, their screams filling the air. Reds had always been avoided, never fought and Remmy momentarily doubted he had the skills or instinct to kill one, but as the girl cried for help, Remmy's mind filled with thoughts of Jessica. Had she cried for help? Begged to be let go before the Reds did whatever they had taken her to do? Anger flared in Remmy's mind and he fought to keep it down. He needed to allow enough to keep his mind sharp, but not enough to overwhelm him. His breathing steadied as he picked up a rock. It was heavy, about the size of a large apple and fit nicely into Remmy's palm. It would have to do.

The Red knelt down and tried to scramble into the wrecked vehicle. It never saw Remmy coming. Never saw the rock crashing into the side of its head.

Remmy swung the rock a few more times, his hand becoming sore, but his fingers unable to put the stone down. The Red stopped moving, but more screams threatened from a rapidly diminishing distance.

Crawling inside the vehicle required Remmy to wade through a tepid pool of the officer's blood. Remmy struggled not to vomit.

"Help!" someone called from the rear of the vehicle. "Please help!"

Remmy wiped sweat from his face and peered through the shattered section of dark glass that separated him from the passengers.

"Come on!" Remmy shouted. "We need to go now! There's not much time!"

The girl shrieked at the red face that looked at her through the divider. Seeing her fear, Remmy suddenly realized that he must have wiped blood across his face.

"I'm not a Red," he yelled. "Am I screaming? We don't have time for this. Come on!"

"My brother," the girl gasped, "he's unconscious. And my mother...my mother..." A sudden deluge of tears cut off the girl's words.

"Your mother is gone. I'm sorry," Remmy said, mustering all the compassion he could give the current situation. "Slide your brother to me and I'll carry him. Can you walk?"

"I think so," the girl said, as she began moving her brother towards the opening.

Remmy grabbed the boy and pulled him out of the wreck. The girl followed close behind.

"Thank you," the girl choked, tears still streaming down her face.

"You're welcome," Remmy grunted as he lifted the boy onto his shoulders. "We need to move, now! Run for the trees." Remmy pointed back towards the copse of old pines.

The Reds' screams grew louder, but Remmy refused to look behind himself. He needed to believe that he would make it to the trees and that he had a chance. If he looked behind him, Remmy knew the Reds would get him.

"Climb!" Remmy yelled as the girl reached the tree.

"Climb?" she asked. "I don't know how...I've never..."

"Just grab the branches and keep going," Remmy coached. "Get up a little and then help me pull him up."

The girl leapt up and began climbing. She was a quick learner. As Remmy hefted the boy into the branches, he noticed that the girl had stopped crying, a look of determination set in her face. The girl looked amazing, like the pictures, Remmy had seen in books at school. She had the confident expression of the statues Remmy had seen of Roman and Greek goddesses. This girl was strong.

The Reds closed in on the trunk of the tree just as Remmy pulled himself into the safety of the tree. They screamed in frustration.

"What do we do now?" the girl asked.

"We wait," Remmy said, knowing that the boy needed medical attention. "Hopefully, if we're quiet, the Reds will wander off. They get distracted pretty easily."

"Thank you," the girl said again.

"You already said that," Remmy smiled. "You don't have to say it twice."

"I'm Cora," she smiled. Another strange feeling blossomed in Cora's chest, this one warm and pleasant. "That's my brother, Xander. Is he going to be okay?"

"I'm Remmy," Remmy grinned. "I think he'll be okay. He just looks banged up." Even though Reds surrounded them, wanting to tear them apart, he couldn't help but smile. This girl was beautiful, unlike any Remmy had ever seen before.

"You're an Emo, aren't you?" Cora asked.

"That going to be a problem?" Remmy smirked.

"No," Cora smiled, "no, it's not."

Assemblyman Eldritch stood in the small foyer that led into the main garden of the Stele house. Being the highest-ranking member of the Citizen's Assembly, he was given the privilege of living there. His family was kept safely inside the city walls and conveniently out of the way at another house. Eldritch could vaguely remember the feelings he had once had for his wife, those intense and overwhelming emotions that drew them together, that were now dulled by his Em-Pak, allowing him to focus single-mindedly on his work. He was important, made decisions that allowed citizens to endure, allowed humanity to endure and some day, so would his children, especially Cora. She showed great potential and would hopefully carry the Eldritch family name further into the pages of history.

With the shackles of his family removed, as well as all feelings of guilt, Eldritch had climbed to a point where he answered to no one, except of course, the ERC. All were accountable to them. But someday, with the proper handling, Cora could find herself the head of the ERC, something that Eldritch had yet to attain.

Eldritch had always marveled at the genius nature of his father's invention. Em-Paks were designed to control emotions, but not the urges behind them. People still strove for power, had the urge to procreate, but lacked the emotions to interpret the importance of these actions beyond continuing the human race. There was no joy in parenthood, as it was simply a means to an end. There needed to be a new generation to carry on the important work of the ERC, so there needed to be children. Parenthood was that simple.

"Sir," an aide said from the doorway. From the way his Em-Pak was chirping repeatedly, Eldritch knew whatever the aide was going to tell him was going to be unpleasant.

"Yes?" Eldritch snapped. "What is it? We've got to film the final address. Is my family prepped for the cameras? I want Cora directly to my right."

"It's about your family, sir," aide said slowly. Eldritch was worried that the man might actually break his Em-Pak from the stress he was currently putting it through.

"Yes, yes," Eldritch grumbled, as he quickly reviewed his talking points. "Make it quick."

"Your family was been delayed, Mr. Eldritch," the aide continued.

"Delayed?" Eldritch growled. His eyes temporarily flared with anger before his Em-Pak beeped, soothing these feelings. "Was there car trouble or something of that nature?"

The aide hesitated. "No sir, it wasn't car trouble. It appears that their limo was ambushed by a pack of Reds."

"Ambushed?" It was Eldritch's Em-Pak's turn to work overtime. "*A pack of Reds?* That's nonsense. They never travel in groups of more than two or three."

"Apparently, sir, they do," the aide answered. "The feed from the limo's cameras showed at least two large groups of Reds closing in on the limo before it crashed. We estimate somewhere between forty to fifty Reds. An ERC recovery team was prepped the second we received the distress call from the limo's guidance system, but I fear they will arrive too late. Your wife appears to have died in the crash as well. Your children have apparently been taken. Teams will be sweeping the area for them as soon as we have your go ahead, sir."

"My wife is dead?" Eldritch asked. "My children have been kidnapped?"

"Yes sir," the aide nodded. "That is what preliminary reports seem to indicate, but there's something else, something unexpected."

"Unexpected?" Eldritch scoffed. "As if an entire pack of Reds is anything but that? What else could be unexpected?"

"Before we lost the camera feed," the aide paused, "well, before it cut out, we saw the image of what appeared to be a young Emo male. We suspect that he was working with the Reds."

"Working with them?" Eldritch asked, his voice betraying a note of concern before his Em-Pak corrected his feelings.

"Yes sir," the aide nodded. "We can't think of why else the Emo would be there. The Reds are just as likely to kill them as they are us, but this boy was somehow at the crash site unharmed."

"I see," Eldritch said slowly. "Cancel the recovery team, but keep me informed of the situation," he barked over his shoulder as he walked towards the large double doors that would let him into the garden.

Some small piece of him screamed for him to feel something, anything at this news. Fear that the Emos and Reds might be working together, sadness over the death of his wife, concern for the safety of his children, but the only thing that Eldritch felt was opportunity.

-7-

The Reds began to wander off as the sun dropped lower into the sky. Remmy could no longer feel his legs or butt and imagined Cora was feeling about the same. Xander had woken up for a brief period and then fallen asleep again.

Cora knew it was bad to let Xander sleep and that he could possibly have a concussion, but he hadn't thrown up or complained and there really was nothing else for him to do. Remmy helped her tie Xander to the trunk of the tree with his belt.

"Looks like only one is left down there," Cora whispered. A shadowy figure grunted from near the base of the tree.

Remmy nodded. "Okay, stay here. I'll deal with the last Red and then we're getting out of here."

"Wait," Cora said reaching out to touch Remmy's arm. A small electrical tingle danced through her fingers and ignited fiery butterflies in her stomach.

"Yeah?" Remmy asked, glancing down at where Cora's hand touched his arm. They had been outside all day, yet her fingers still felt warm.

"Oh, um," Cora mumbled as she jerked her hand back, trying to make it look natural, but failing miserably. "Do you think it's a good idea to go and fight that Red?"

"Good idea?" Remmy chuckled. "No, it's a terrible one, but I'm open to other suggestions if you got any."

"Can't we just wait for someone to come and get us? I'm sure my father will send someone soon," Cora offered, but immediately realized how badly that would end for Remmy.

"Your father will send someone?" Remmy asked. He knew this girl had to be the child of someone important, but hadn't stopped to consider it yet. "Who are you?"

"Me?" Cora asked, realizing that her comment had given more away than she had intended. Her heart hammered in her chest. "I'm no one. I was just saying that I thought all vehicles had an emergency call if they crashed. I thought maybe my father would have known by now and sent help."

"No offense," Remmy smirked, "but don't you think they'd be here already if they were coming? Besides, I'm not waiting around for the ERC to show up. I'd rather take my chances with the Red. Stay here, okay?"

Cora shook her head yes, but the idea of Remmy leaving her filled with a strange swirling sensation somewhat like the time she had ridden a roller coaster at the amusement park in the Stele, but even that had felt more controlled than this. Her mind and body were in revolt and Cora had no idea why. She was in awe of Remmy's bravery and selflessness and also terrified by the prospect of him never coming back.

"Be careful," Cora whispered as Remmy began quietly moving lower.

Remmy paused to look up and smile. Why was this girl making him smile so much and at such inappropriate times? He needed to focus.

The Red paced around the base of the tree, a crude blade in its left hand. Remmy had no idea how he was going to handle this one. The first Red had been unarmed and distracted.

A large pinecone brushed Remmy's cheek as he hovered on the branch above the Red. At first, he irately slapped it away, but then thought better and grabbed it. A pinecone was a poor weapon against a Red, but maybe he could still find some use for it.

Remmy pitched the pinecone around the other side of the tree. It made a faint rustling were it landed in some tangled underbrush and leaves. The Red's head snapped towards the sound and it dropped lower to the ground, flattening itself like the jungle cats Remmy had seen in his schoolbooks. This was what he was hoping for.

As the Red moved towards the sound, Remmy aimed his feet and leapt off the branch. His boots landed squarely in the middle of the Red's back. A sickening crunch sounded from the Red's back, followed by its angry screams. It flailed the knife, but its legs refused to move.

Seeing that Remmy had incapacitated the Red, Cora unstrapped Xander and began moving out of the tree. She dropped to the ground just behind Remmy.

"Come on," Cora hissed. "Let's get out of here before anymore Reds show up."

"We can't leave yet," Remmy said, a sad look in his eyes. "We can't leave her like this."

"Her?" Cora almost cried. "Remmy it's a Red, a monster. It would have killed us if it got the chance, maybe worse."

"She's not a monster," Remmy said softly. "She's just sick. It's not her fault." Remmy searched the ground for a rock, but found none. "Cora, go wait for me over by those trees, please."

"Remmy," Cora began to argue, but saw that he had already made up his mind. "Okay."

Cora watched as Remmy stepped down on the Red's arm and pulled the knife free. It was growing dark, but she could still make out his silhouette as he knelt down on the Red's shoulders, pinning it to the ground. It screamed ferociously as Remmy leaned forward and made a quick motion with his arm. The Red fell silent.

"Let's go," Remmy said, tears in his eyes.

Cora could feel her heart breaking for Remmy, could feel the jagged shards of it travel through her body tearing her apart. She felt sick, but it was nothing like the colds or illnesses she had suffered before. This was worse.

"I'm sorry you had to do that, Remmy," she offered, hoping it might help.

"Yeah," Remmy muttered, "me too, but it couldn't be helped. Let's go, I'm sure everyone back at my camp is worried."

"You're taking us there?" Cora gasped. "Is that safe?"

"For who?" Remmy laughed, "You or us?"

Cora felt waves of heat on her face, could feel the prickle on the back of her neck. Had she just insulted Remmy?

"I just meant that, well, I mean," Cora struggled for the words.

"Don't worry about it," Remmy grinned. "We need to get your brother checked out and my camp is the closest place, so that's where we're going."

Cora nodded. As Remmy moved to pick up Xander, his bare arm brushed against Cora's. Millions of tiny bolts danced through her skin, goose bumps involuntarily rising on her arms.

"You okay?" Remmy asked.

"Yeah, sure," Cora nodded, "I'm fine." But the truth was that she wasn't. Cora knew something was wrong with her. Something had happened.

The realization that she had spent the entire day in a tree with a strange and exciting boy, surrounded by Reds and not once heard her Em-Pak's telltale beep dawned on Cora.

"Let's go," Remmy smiled and started into the woods. Cora followed close behind. Something was definitely wrong, something terrible and life altering. With trembling fingers, Cora gingerly touched the back of her neck. The Em-Pak was still there, still felt like it always had, but it had spent the entire day silent. Something was very wrong and Cora was beginning to think that she might enjoy it.

-8-

"Despite our best efforts and the tireless work of the ERC, the Red threat has reemerged even more dangerous. It is with great concern that I report the kidnapping of my children. It is with an even deeper sadness that I report the passing of my wife, as well as an ERC officer who fought valiantly to protect my family."

Assemblyman Eldritch paused and let his speech sink in. It was strange to say "an even deeper sadness" about the death of his wife because the truth was he felt nothing, least of all sadness. But the expression was something that citizens had clung to from the old times. It was also an expression that Eldritch hoped would soon be forgotten. So many words wasted on sentimentality and ceremony.

Citizens had expected the annual speech commemorating the work of the elder Samuel Eldritch and his invention of the Em-Pak. Assemblyman Eldritch's words shocked them. He could almost hear Em-Paks citywide chirping loudly, doing their best to correct the fear that he was doing his best to foster.

The citizens had become complacent, had come to believe that the worst of times had passed and that belief was dangerous. They needed to be reminded why they needed the Assembly and the ERC. Too much safety, too much freedom, those were the building blocks of independent thought. Eldritch was currently doing his best to scatter those blocks, to make citizens remember why they needed him.

"And now good citizens, I must ask you to put aside your concerns for my family. Please rest assured that the ERC is doing everything in its power to rescue my children and punish those responsible for the death of my beloved wife. I ask you to put those concerns aside, because an even greater threat darkens our doorways, an even more malignant cancer has taken root outside the walls of our cities."

The crowd began to shift uncomfortably at what Eldritch was preparing to unveil. There would undoubtedly be some feathers ruffled at the ERC, but with his family planted at the center of this debacle, Eldritch could easily smooth things over. The ERC would need him, would need his family as a rallying call to the citizenry. Once this was over, Eldritch could practically vote himself in as the head of the ERC – something he had previously felt slipping through his fingers.

A few beeps from Em-Paks attached to those citizens in the front row shook Eldritch from his thoughts. He smiled as he listened to the faint chirps of the Em-Paks. His own quickly answered the call, correcting his own feelings. A few more Em-Paks sounded in the crowd. They were scared. That was good. It was time for Eldritch to drop a bomb and solidify his place.

"We have survived much, sacrificed much to secure our place in this world. We have faced the virus, conquered it with my father's invention of the Em-Pak. We have significantly cut down on the numbers of those monstrous, mindless Reds that threatened our children, our way of life. But even this has not been enough. No, good citizens, it is our fellow man who currently poses the greatest danger to us. Those misguided few that choose to live without Em-Paks. I speak of Emos of course. They were once thought to be little more than the seeds of future Reds, but now they have proven themselves to be something far worse, something far more dangerous. The Emos have joined forces with the Reds to destroy all of our hard work. My family's blood was the first drawn in this new war and I intend to ensure that it will be the last! My family will not have suffered in vain! We must punish these terrorists! It is our duty and will be my honor to wipe the Emos and Reds from the face of this earth!"

The citizens began to cheer and clap, though their eyes were blank and glassy. They were well trained. Eldritch had them exactly where he wanted them.

"Following this speech, I will be going directly to the ERC Council to petition for increased patrols, increased funding and increased protection! I will ensure that no family suffers as mine has. I will ensure that you are safe! That is the legacy of the Eldritch name! It is my birthright, a torch passed on to me by my father and my honor to carry! With your support, good citizens, I will lead us through these dark times and into the future that we have all dreamed of, the future that is rightfully ours!"

Walking back through the double doors and into the Assembly House, Eldritch could still hear the crowd cheering. He momentarily felt a flood of pride before his Em-Pak chirped loudly and returned him to baseline. Before the implantation of his Em-Pak, a speech like that would have made Eldritch smile for days. Now, he was allowed a few fleeting seconds of pride before it was lost to the device's influence.

"Um, sir," his aide hesitated, "the ERC Council phoned at the conclusion of your speech. They have requested your presence at their office, right away."

"Splendid," Eldritch nodded. "Please ready the car. I'll be going there right away."

"Splendid?" the aide repeated, confused. A request to appear before the ERC Council was many things, but splendid surely was not one of them.

"Yes," Eldritch nodded, "splendid, indeed. Now let's not dawdle. Bring the car around and notify the ERC that I'll be arriving shortly."

-9-

Noises sounded softly throughout the forest. Remmy appeared unfazed by them as he carried a semi-conscious Xander over his shoulders. Cora, on the other hand, was overwhelmed. She had been to city parks, the best city parks, reserved only for those with money and political connections, but she had never experienced nature like this. She had heard dozens of birds sing, but had never felt their songs. Never had they resonated within her being, echoing to some long lost poetic yearning. Cora was amazed that such a few simple notes could create such a reaction.

After a second time, tripping over tree roots, Cora decided that she had better find some way to focus or Remmy would be carrying her too.

"Are you sure it's okay to bring us back?" Cora asked. A strange tightness had wound itself around her guts after Remmy told them where he was taking them. She was unsure of what it meant, but could barely contain the onslaught of questions that filled her mind. "I mean, are you sure no one will get upset?"

"Upset?" Remmy shrugged, eliciting a mumble from Xander, "I don't know. Don't really care either. There was no other choice. Everyone is just going to have to deal with it."

Was it really that simple Cora wondered? *Everyone is just going to have to deal with it?* Could it really be possible to live your life with little concern for the reactions of others? Cora had spent her entire life in the spotlight, in front of cameras, judged by everyone, especially her father. But Remmy was different. He appeared to care little for what others thought of him and it gave him lightness, a certain degree of freedom that Cora was beginning to desire for herself.

"I guess so," Cora answered. "But what about the ERC?"

"What about them?" Remmy grunted. "It's not like I haven't lived my entire life hiding from them and looking over my shoulder. The ERC trying to kill Emos is not exactly news to anyone I know."

"They try to kill you?" Cora asked, suddenly realizing what her father's use of the words "unacceptable" and "unsuitable" actually meant. It was true that all citizens knew that ERC patrols were trying to exterminate the threats posed from Emos, but Cora, like all those with an Em-Pak, had lacked the ability to feel compassion and empathy. Stopping, to think of the Emos as actual people, like *Remmy*, sent waves of nausea roiling through Cora's gut. She stumbled and grabbed a nearby tree, trying to steady herself.

"Cora?" Remmy asked, panic swelling in his words. "Cora, are you okay?" He set Xander down and rushed to Cora's side.

"I...I...think so...I'm not..." Cora's words were cut short by a violent burst of vomit. She collapsed to the ground, her head swimming and the world appearing to spin. "Remmy," Cora said weakly. "Remmy, something's wrong?" Cora struggled to steady herself, but her body revolted against her.

"Cora?" Remmy cried as she fell to the ground. Her eyes fluttered, her breathing slowed and Cora stopped moving. Remmy shook her shoulders. "Cora! Wake up, Cora!" Remmy quickly checked Cora's breathing. It was shallow and slow, but still there.

"Sorry, man," Remmy muttered as he sprinted past Xander. The boy was slightly conscious. Remmy hoped he wouldn't wake up in the middle of the woods with no idea where he was, but there was no way, Remmy could carry them both and surely no way, he could run with Xander on his shoulders.

The woods blurred as Remmy pushed his legs to move faster and faster. He dodged rocks and sprang over downed logs, never slowing down or stumbling. Cora was all he could see. What was it about her? She filled his mind's eye, allowing his brain to focus on nothing but thoughts of her. Cora's image willed him to move faster, and ignore the burning in his legs and lungs. He just needed to keep going. He needed to save Cora.

-10-

The ERC had numerous offices, but none as imposing as the central headquarters located in the Stele. Most citizens gave the gray stone building a wide berth, rightly choosing to avoid contact with ERC officers and officials. Windows, tinted silver, adorned the higher officers, watching over the citizens like flat rectangular reptilian eyes. Heavy metal doors and a handful of ERC officers guarded the front of the building, but both currently stood to the side to allow Assemblyman Eldritch to enter.

The early chaos of the virus created a power vacuum. Governments crumbled and were trampled under the feet of the Reds. Many politicians, fragile creatures that they were, succumbed to the virus and tore one another apart. People were in a state of panic, fearing that the world was quickly coming to an end. In those times, free of Em-Paks, people had the ability and common sense to feel afraid, and feel worried, but also the arrogance to ignore the true root of the virus. Across this frothing, turbulent sea of blood, a light shone, a beacon of hope. Perhaps more importantly, it was a solution that required no accountability or personal responsibility. People were told they were victims and that nature had simply turned against them and unleashed the virus. Their way of life, their selfishness and disregard for their fellow man had plowed the fields in which the virus' seed took root, but it surely was not their fault. Surely, there had to be some explanation that pointed fingers somewhere else. The Em-Pak cured humans of all of these concerns.

With the removal of one's emotions, there no longer remained a reason to question one's actions, especially those of the past. With no sense of the past, all that remained was for someone to articulate a clear vision of the future. The ERC emerged to fill this void. Crippled governments yielded to the ERC, trading power for Em-Paks and security.

Eldritch had been summoned to appear before the ERC Council very few times, which was probably why he had been allowed to climb such lofty political heights. What he had just done, the speech he had given, flew in the face of everything the

34

ERC stood for. He had been tasked with giving a speech to remind citizens of why they needed the ERC, why they needed to be compliant. Eldritch's words were intended to inspire fear, or at least what passed for fear where Em-Paks were concerned. He felt fairly certain that this meeting was not going to go well, but found strength in the fact that he had placed his family at the epicenter of this new threat. He made himself, his kidnapped children and his dead wife the symbols behind which citizens could rally. Even the ERC couldn't ignore that or squander the opportunity.

"Sit," a voice boomed as Eldritch walked into the room. Shadows obscured the members of the ERC Council. Their mission was more important than a single person was. It had been decided that, all members would remain hidden, thus eliminating the citizen's urge to choose one leader over another. Priority was given to none, but power secured by all.

The room was lit only by a large spotlight, shining directly into Eldritch's eyes, preventing him from seeing much of anything. It communicated the ERC Council's desire to let all citizens know, even Assembly members that they were being watched at all times. Eldritch lowered himself into the high backed leather chair. The red leather and brass fasteners shone under the intense light, providing a stark contrast to the bland grayness of the room. Eldritch knew that even this was intentional, another ERC ploy to make the person feel singled out. His Em-Pak remained silent.

"Assemblyman Eldritch, you were provided with an ERC approved speech for this event," the voice echoed, "were you not?"

"That is true," Eldritch nodded.

"Yet, you chose to disregard this speech and *improvise*," the faceless members of the ERC accused. To improvise was to employ independent thought, to make a decision that may not be in the best interest of all citizens. Independence was dangerous and rooted in self-motivating emotions. These insidious and traitorous actions would not be tolerated, especially by a figurehead the likes of Eldritch.

"That is also true," Eldritch admitted. He knew they thrived on fear, pushed citizens to incriminate themselves. He was going to give them nothing. They would have to *ask* for his reasons.

"And would you care to tell us why?" a member of the ERC Council demanded, her words soaked in venom.

"The citizens have become complacent," Eldritch said coolly.

"Complacency is not a problem, Assemblyman," a faceless Council member snapped. "A complacent population is a docile one. To inspire fear is to create chaos. Chaos breeds insurrection and allows the virus to return. It will not be tolerated."

"I respectfully disagree," Eldritch smirked. "Chaos is not something the citizens are accustomed to, but complacency is. Allowing the citizens to remain complacent is dangerous. It gives them time to think, but more importantly, time to forget. Time to forget why they need us, and why they need you." Eldritch's words were tantamount to heresy, but he had weighed the risks and he knew how to play this situation to his benefit.

Muffled voices communicated behind shielded microphones.

"Continue," the ERC Council commanded. Eldritch couldn't help but smile. The ERC Council members knew he was right. They saw his rationale. Now, all that remained was to drive his point home and secure his future position.

"As I was saying," Eldritch continued, "the citizens have been allowed to feel too safe and that is dangerous. If they forget what they need us to protect them from, then they may very well begin to feel that they no longer need us. We will see a dramatic rise in emotional treason and ultimately a resurgence of the virus and the Reds, the likes of which we have never seen. Now I realize that I gave a speech that was not ERC approved, but I felt it prudent to act before news of my family reached the populous. We needed to ensure that we controlled the distribution and spin of this bit of information to ensure that the information could be used to strengthen our position, not to weaken it."

"Is this why you called off the ERC recovery team?" the Council boomed.

"I called them off because they would have done their job too well and recovered my children," Eldritch admitted. "They would have brought them back and this entire incident would soon be forgotten."

"You're willing to sacrifice your son and daughter to the Reds to make this point?" The ERC Council's words held no accusation, rather were simply a point of clarification.

"We all must be willing to sacrifice for the greater good," Eldritch nodded. "Of course, no sacrifice should be made without note."

"Of course," the voice responded. "So what exactly do you propose we do to ensure that the citizens are kept aware of their need of us?"

"Nothing," Eldritch grinned. His Em-Pak chirped, correcting his smug sense of self-satisfaction.

"Nothing?" the ERC barked.

"Exactly," Eldritch replied. "We have done too much already, have spoiled the citizens. I propose that we allow the virus and Reds to creep back, just ever so slightly into some of the outer cities, just enough to remind the citizens that they are only safe because we make them such. Once that point is driven home and the citizens have been properly educated regarding the new threat posed by the Red and Emo collaboration, we will have total control. Emotional treason will cease and the herd will be ready to be led once again."

"This can be controlled?" the ERC asked.

"Of course," Eldritch smiled. "I'll personally oversee a team of ERC officers that will ensure the situation never gets out of hand."

"And your children?" the ERC asked, not out of concern, but more so to clarify Eldritch's motivations.

"If they're recovered," Eldritch shrugged, "then we'll use them as the new mascots for this campaign, as something the citizens can rally behind."

"And if they are not?"

"If they're not recovered," Eldritch paused, "well, then they'll become martyrs, examples for all young citizens to follow."

"This is..." the ERC Council paused, "acceptable. You may leave, but do not make the mistake of acting without our approval again."

"Of course," Eldritch bowed slightly, "never again." His Em-Pak beeped three more times before he reached the door. He had gotten exactly what he wanted. Now with a small army at his disposal and the ERC appearing to have allowed the virus to return, Eldritch could begin to lay the foundation of his new kingdom. He had once thought that leading the ERC was the highest he could hope to climb in his political career, but as he relaxed in the plush seats of his limo, he decided that it would be far more satisfying to replace them.

-11-

People had already begun frantically to pack their cars as Remmy tore into the middle of the camp. His disappearance and now frenzied reappearance led the other Emos to believe that the ERC couldn't be far behind.

"Remmy!" his mother cried as he collapsed against the side of the family jeep. "Where have you been? Are you okay? Was it the ERC? Remmy? Do we need to go? Answer me right now!"

"I would," Remmy panted, "if you ever stopped to take a breath."

"Damn it, Remmy," his father snapped. "Where the hell have you been? You don't show up for school and disappear for the half the day. We thought the worst."

"I got trapped in a tree," Remmy said, slowly catching his breath, "but that doesn't matter. I saw a huge group of Reds attack a car. It crashed and I pulled two kids from the wreck, but they're hurt and out in the woods." Remmy knew that he was leaving out the part about the car being an ERC vehicle and the kids being fitted with Em-Paks, but he needed people to act. Cora's life was depending on him. ERC or not, Remmy could tell that Cora was a good person.

"Children?" Remmy's mother gasped.

"A group of Reds?" his father asked. He reached into the back of the jeep and pulled out his old hunting rifle. "That makes no sense. They never travel in groups of more than two or three."

"I know," Remmy answered, "but I'm telling you, Dad, that there were at least forty of them. They attacked the car, like they had planned it or something."

"Planned?" Remmy's father repeated. That made no sense. The Reds were wild, operated on instinct. True, they would set crude traps to snare Emos, but they had never been organized.

"It was planned," Remmy said adamantly. "They came at the car in two groups. The one from the back chased the car towards the group in the front. Most of them were ripped up in the crash, but they had a third group coming in. I had to pull the kids out

39

quick, before they got there. No one else was left. We were chased, so I had them hide in a tree. I had to silence two Reds."

"You silenced two Reds?" Remmy's father asked, his face a mask of concern. "Are you okay?"

"Yeah," Remmy said quietly, remembering what he had done. "I'm okay. I didn't have a choice." He would do what was required to protect people, but he still struggled to rationalize taking a life.

"Of course not," Remmy's mother added, pulling her son into a bear hug. "You did what you had to do. Now get in the jeep and go get those children. We can't just leave them out there. I'll tell the others to get the doctor."

Other Emos gathered close to hear Remmy's story. The idea of a pack of Reds sent fear coursing through each of them, but the thought of two injured children, alone in the woods galvanized their resolve. Four cars, loaded with Emos, rolled out of the camp in a tight line. Remmy and his father led the way in the jeep.

Remmy gripped the dashboard and quietly willed his father to drive faster. He knew what was wrong with Xander, that was obvious, but Cora had seemed fine and then suddenly just fallen ill. Could she had been injured in the crash and not realized it? Could it be something worse? Remmy hoped that whatever it was, the doctor would be able to help her. He had just met her, just learned that she existed could she really be taken away so soon? That seemed so cruel, so unfair. If life had taught Remmy nothing else, it was that, yes, she could. Life cared little for what was fair.

"Dad?" Remmy asked, his voice raw.

"We'll get there, Rem," his father replied and pushed the gas pedal closer to the floor.

-12-

The Eldritch house was empty. The servants were sent home early, and a dinner left to cool in the oven slowly. Assemblyman Eldritch had always insisted upon a tidy, shipshape home that operated with the precision of a Swiss watch, but now it seemed empty, completely silent and hollow. It was, in one word, perfect.

Moving from room to room, Eldritch marveled at the silence. At one point in his early life, a house like this would have been disconcerting, a reason for alarm. Now though, Em-Pak firmly implanted, Eldritch found the house absolutely wonderful. There were no distractions; no little daily duties that required his attention. All he was left with were his thoughts and plans. The Em-Pak truly was an amazing invention. It was a shame that his father had been taken by the Reds before he could have furthered his invention, found some way to make it even better. But that was the puzzle left for Eldritch to solve, simply another piece to fit into his plan.

Spreading his father's notes across the polished mahogany dining room table, Eldritch poured over the neatly written handwriting in the margins, pondering the bits of half-finished thoughts that his father left for him to piece together. He had previously attempted to find some answer in these papers, some scrap of unrealized greatness for him to grab, but there had always been the demands of the ERC and family. Neither required his emotional investment. Those days were long since buried by his Em-Pak, but they still ate large amounts of his time. Now, with the ERC in his pocket and his family little more than a politically valuable memory, Eldritch was free to spend time as he saw fit.

The cell phone on the table began to vibrate and clatter across the polished wood.

"Yes?" Eldritch snapped. He felt heat rise on the back of his neck and then quickly dissipate under his Em-Pak's influence.

"Sir?" it was Eldritch's aide. "Sorry to bother you, sir, but there's been a recent development."

"And that would be?" Eldritch asked, only half listening as he looked over his father's notes.

"It appears that some citizens, following your speech, went looking for Emos in their own neighborhoods," the aide reported. "It's still unclear as to whether or not they actually found any citizens who had removed their Em-Paks, but they are rioting, pulling people out of their homes."

"Rioting?" Eldritch smiled, his Em-Pak chirped.

"Yes sir," the aide continued. "There are similar reports coming from the outer cities, those with less of an ERC presence. It appears that the citizens do not want to wait for ERC officers to arrive to secure the cities. The situation is quickly becoming unmanageable."

"This is excellent," Eldritch nodded. "Inform the local ERC offices to do what they can to control the damage to structures, but have the heads of all those offices report directly to me, as per ERC Council orders."

"Yes sir," his aide responded, unsure of what he was really agreeing to.

"Excellent," Eldritch repeated to himself. If the citizens were becoming unruly, that would open the cities up to infection. A flare up in the outer cities would certainly gain the attention of those richer, more influential citizens living in the Stele.

The riots would undoubtedly cause the chaos that Eldritch sought, but even more importantly, citizens fighting one another would lead to damaged Em-Paks and ultimately, Reds within the city walls. In the chaos and carnage, an Eldritch would once again emerge to rescue humanity.

Now all that remained was to figure out how Eldritch was going to do this before the pandemonium he created destroyed the very thing he sought to control.

-13-

Bits of sunlight and conversation filtered in through the loose flaps of the tent. Cora's entire body felt like it had been run over by a transport, which considering the last few days probably wasn't too inaccurate.

"You realize where we are, don't you?" Xander asked, his eyes narrow and feet hanging off the edge of a green canvas cot. A large bruise had blossomed on the side of his right arm. Another smaller one darkened the corner of his left eye, but he otherwise appeared to be okay.

"We're in Remmy's camp," Cora groaned as she pushed herself up to sitting. "He pulled us out of the car wreck."

"He's an Emo," Xander muttered. "We're in an Emo camp, a terrorist camp."

"He saved you," Cora snapped. "If it hadn't been for that Emo, you would've been torn apart by the Reds."

"The ERC would have saved us," Xander argued. "Father would have sent a recovery team. He probably did. They probably arrived and couldn't find us because of your little friend, *Remmy*." Xander said his name as if it tasted foul upon his tongue. "Now we're stuck here in some terrorist camp and father must think the worst."

"Father?" Cora snorted. Something acidic and fiery bloomed in her gut. It was unpleasant, but felt right, felt appropriate. "Are you really that naïve, Xander? If father wanted to save us, he would have. While you were busy passing out, Remmy dragged you up into a tree where we had to spend the entire day because of the Reds. He killed two of them to keep us safe, but no one from the ERC showed up, least of all father."

Cora had spent the last few days piecing together the events surrounding the crash. Remmy had saved them, her father had apparently done nothing and her mother was dead. Cora felt an overwhelming force crushing down upon her shoulders. She could feel the weight of these events reshaping her life, but why didn't Xander? How was he so complacent? The thoughts ricocheted through Cora's mind like wild bullets. She grasped for them, trying to make sense, but her body still felt like it was revolting, still out of control.

Breathing out deeply and running her fingers backwards through her hair Cora tried to calm herself. This nervous habit would sometimes show up, but quickly be erased with one tinny bleep of her Em-Pak. *Her Em-Pak!* Cora's mind screamed as her fingers felt the large rectangular bandage on the back of her neck. The small rise of her Em-Pak, something that had become as familiar as a freckle, was gone. Her Em-Pak had been removed!

"Yup," Xander smiled coldly. "They removed your Em-Pak, but left mine on for some reason. But your Em-Pak is gone, Cora. You're guilty of emotional treason."

"How can I be guilty of something I didn't do?" Cora almost cried. Tears welled in her eyes. This was a death sentence.

"Doesn't matter," Xander shrugged. "It's gone, and that's a crime, so you're guilty. This will look very bad for father, a close family member committing a high crime. Jeez, Cora, you really are an idiot. You didn't even stop to think about how what you were doing could impact father's career."

"Father's career?" Cora snapped, that feeling deep in her gut giving her words a sharp edge. "His career? Are you serious, Xander? We could have died! Mother did! Doesn't that matter to you? Don't you care?"

"Mother's death is...regrettable," Xander responded. His Em-Pak beeped. "Ours would have been as well, but I'm sure the ERC and the citizens won't allow mother's sacrifice to have occurred in vain."

"Xander, you can't possibly think that this situation should be used as propaganda," Cora admonished. "Please tell me that you don't think that."

"Why shouldn't I?" Xander asked. "Every situation offers an advantage if one looks closely enough. Father taught me that. It's disappointing that you wouldn't have figured that out for yourself. Honestly, I don't know what he was thinking, grooming you instead of me."

"Enough!" Cora growled. "Xander, you have an answer for everything, huh? So why don't you tell me what we should do."

"Leave, find the nearest ERC office and turn all of these terrorists in," Xander stated matter-of-factly. "Then you can plead for mercy. Maybe Father will convince the ERC to kill you quickly."

"Kill me?" Cora asked. Her words were sharp and painful in her mouth.

"You committed emotional treason," Xander shrugged. "I don't really see how this could end differently. Maybe if you help me turn in these terrorists the ERC will grant you exile or imprisonment. Of course, that's only delaying the inevitable because the virus will take you now that your Em-Pak is gone."

"Don't even think about it," Cora threatened. With the Em-Pak gone, a swirling mix of emotions roiled through her. She wanted so badly for Xander to share her hope for a new life, for a second chance outside of the city walls, but he was too myopic, too eager to prove himself to their father. There was no way she could convince him, even if she removed his Em-Pak.

"Oh please," Xander snorted. "Or what, Cora? You'll get mad? Please do. Then not only will father have a terrorist in the family, but a Red as well. Having his daughter cleaned would really drive up his approval ratings. Maybe I'd be able to do it? Publicly killing a monster could really lay some groundwork for me get into the ERC."

Before she knew what she was doing, Cora lunged across the tent and slammed Xander down against the cot. His eyes remained calm and steady, his face expressionless. The beeping of his Em-Pak could be heard beneath Cora's angry breathing.

"You do anything, *anything* to threaten Remmy," Cora snarled, "and I'll show you a freaking monster!"

"Cora, let him go," Remmy's voice commanded. His tone was even and firm, but laced with concern. "Take a few deep breaths. Go in through your nose and out through your mouth. Focus on something happy." Remmy realized that Cora might not have a happy memory, might not even know what happy was. Cora most likely didn't have any memories tied to emotions, but he needed to calm her down.

"But he…" Cora protested. "He said he was going to…"

"I heard him," Remmy nodded. "But it's not his fault. It's the Em-Pak. He doesn't know what he's saying."

"Please," Xander snorted. "I don't need some filthy Emo to come to my rescue."

"You did before," Remmy smirked, "when you were passed out in the wreck about to be torn apart by a Red. Forget pretty quickly, huh?"

"Next time, feel free to leave me," Xander answered. "My death will do more for Father's cause than spending the rest of my life as a terrorist's prisoner."

"Terrorist?" Remmy chuckled. "You're so twisted up by your Em-Pak that you don't know what the hell you're saying. Man, look around. Do you see any terrorists? These are just regular people trying to survive. If anyone is peddling terror around here it's the ERC, not us."

"Don't even bother," Cora snapped. Her shoulders heaved with short breaths, but she let Xander fall back onto the cot. What had she just done? She felt something towards Xander, something dark and menacing, but it was more than that. Underneath those strange feelings were even stranger ones. He was her little brother. That meant something, meant she should protect him, even from himself.

"Let him stay here if he wants," Remmy replied. "Come on. I want to show you something."

"Aren't you worried that he'll escape and report all of you to the ERC?" Cora hesitated.

"He's free to walk around camp," Remmy answered, "but the guards aren't going to let him leave unsupervised. I'm sorry, Xander, but with your Em-Pak still functioning it's just too risky not to notify the watch. If you need anything, just ask, okay? Everyone is here to help."

"I'm sure," Xander glared. "The nicest kidnappers in the world, right? I hope you're not waiting for me to go all Patty Hearst like my sister, because that's going to happen."

"Didn't think it would," Remmy answered. "But you're wrong man. We're not kidnapping you. As soon as we can find a way to safely return you to your father, we'll do it."

"Top priority, I'm sure," Xander scoffed as he slumped back onto his cot.

"Come on, Cora," Remmy said, holding the flap of the tent open. "There's someone I want you to meet."

-14-

Riots flared up in the outer cities and spread with the ferocity of a wildfire. Eldritch wondered how long he should allow this to continue before he stepped in and saved the citizens. He spent days locked away in the solitude of his house, pouring over his father's notes and looking for some way to solidify his position as second generation savior to humanity. So far, a few ideas appeared promising, but nothing definite.

Eldritch needed to think fast. The ERC was growing impatient, demanding results and the violence was spreading faster than Eldritch had anticipated. Of course, he had expected the citizens to turn on one another, and tear apart anything that appeared different, but this was beyond expectations. The Em-Paks must have suppressed a great deal more of the citizens' natural desire to crush their neighbors than Eldritch had thought. Now, though, with a logical excuse, instead of an emotional one, the citizens were free to terrorize and riot as they pleased. Furthermore, their Em-Pak's influence ensured that they could do so without a second thought or pang of guilt.

However, with each riot a new crop of Reds were created. Eldritch was careful to have his ERC officers on standby to clean up the mess, but was also careful to allow the insanity to last long enough to make his point. The Emos, on the other hand, were proving to be less reliable than the citizens and Reds.

Eldritch watched the video from his family's accident and a young Emo clearly arrives at the wreck and takes Cora and Xander. The boy had to be working with the Reds. How else could he have gotten so close without being torn apart?

Punching a few keys on his computer, Eldritch cued the video from the accident and transferred it to the large screen mounted on his wall. He began sorting through the feed shot by shot. The officer can be seen climbing out. Then a scream is heard. He drops to the ground near the camera, obscuring most of the view. A Red steps over the officer's body. Its feet are visible as it tries to clamber through the shattered limo window. Moments later, the boy appears and…

"Damn it," Eldritch seethed and paused the video. His Em-Pak began beeping furiously. The anger slowly melted from his body. Watching the recording closely, Eldritch spied what looked like a rock dropped to the ground. What he had once thought was the boy coming to assist the Red, now looked like him killing it with the damn stone. The Red's legs stopped moving just before the feed cut out. The damn Emo must have *saved* his children, not kidnapped them. If this got out, Eldritch would be finished. The ERC would make him disappear and there was no telling how the citizens would respond to the information, especially with their newfound sense of logical rebellion.

Eldritch had to spin this, and get it under control. The citizens, and more importantly the ERC, needed to believe that the Reds and Emos were working in conjunction. The idea of this new threat was the linchpin to Eldritch's entire plan, without it, things would fall apart.

Groaning loudly, Eldritch turned his attention back to his father's notes. A few small scribbles were on the last few pages, something he must have been working on just before he died. Eldritch shifted the notes towards the light of his desk lamp and looked closer. The carefully written words read like both his death sentence and salvation:

"I have come to realize that the Em-Paks have side effects." The notes began. *"These devices should only be viewed as a temporary solution to the dangers of the virus and Reds. The Em-Paks are designed to suppress emotions and control them, but they do not erase them completely. Logically, I knew that these devices were temporary. It would be prudent to cycle them. Implantation in the current generation would serve to save society, but the Em-Pak is not permanent. Eventually, we will need to learn to control our emotional responses independent of these devices. Future generations should have an Em-Pak implanted at birth, but removed following proper emotional training and the advent of adulthood. It would be foolhardy and dangerous to think that the Em-Paks are a vaccine. Like all technology, they have limits. My preliminary experiments seem to indicate that given an overly emotional situation, the Em-Pak will malfunction and do the opposite of what is was intended to do. This sudden onslaught of*

emotions would surely overwhelm the citizens and lead to infection. I shudder to think what would occur in this situation, large pockets of the virus cropping up and ultimately cities overrun with Reds. To that end, I have programmed an override into the design of the Em-Pak. Given the correct sequencing code, the devices can be either shut down or magnified. It is my hope that the ERC will only use this failsafe in the direst of situations."

Eldritch sneered at the notes. His own father lacked faith and vision. What would people think if this was ever made public? The populous could not be trusted to live without Em-Paks. Could his father really have been that naïve?

"My hopes are that once the Em-Paks have controlled the initial outbreaks of the virus and the cities made safe from Reds that citizens will learn to control their emotions through natural means. We must become responsible for our actions and emotions. It is my theory that the virus is rooted in negative emotions, but that we as a society have reached a point where we can no longer tell the difference between love and hate. These two emotions have become so intertwined that we now lack the ability to distinguish one from other. We must seek to transcend our selfishness and recapture the essence of humanity now that we have seen what living without compassion brings. My hope is that the Em-Pak will allow us to do so. Tomorrow, I will bring my results before the ERC as well as my plan to slowly wean the populous from my invention in the future."

"The ERC knows?" Eldritch muttered. "They know that the Em-Paks could ultimately fail? Interesting…" The failsafe that his father had installed could be used to either increase the Em-Pak influence or to completely turn them off. This was exactly what Eldritch had been looking for. Now all that remained was to find some way to involve the Emos.

Grabbing his phone, Eldritch called his aide.

"Yes sir?" the aide mumbled, it was after one a.m.

"Wake up!" Eldritch demanded. "Damn it, wake up, right now!"

"I am, sir," the aide lied. "I'm up, sir."

"It's time to call in the team," Eldritch snapped.

"Sir?" the aide questioned, as if he were unsure of what he had just been told to do. "I thought we were only going to do that in the event of an emergency."

"Are you questioning my orders?" Eldritch growled. He could almost hear his aide's Em-Pak chirp. "Turn on your damn television. Does that look like anything other than an emergency?"

"No, absolutely not, sir. I mean, yes sir, it does," the aide answered quickly. "I'll inform the team to make ready."

"Very good," Eldritch smiled. "Tell Captain Ortiz to make sure that the orders are clear. They are not there to assist the citizens. This may seem confusing, but it is for the greater good. These loyal men will follow my orders, so make them clear. They are to infiltrate the cities as Emos. Do not shoot the Reds. Understood?"

"Yes sir," the aide answered. "And your orders beyond that?"

"Create chaos," Eldritch said coolly. "Tell them to have fun."

-15-

"Where are we going?" Cora asked as she and Remmy walked through the Emo camp. Cora was surrounded with new, overwhelming sights, things she had never known to exist. Deceptively simple actions were alien and incredible. A mother cradled a tiny baby, gently rocking and singing to it as it cooed. A group of dirt speckled children played an intense game that appeared to involve little more than tagging another person and remaining still until someone else tagged them. People smiled and laughed. Life, one that Cora had never known to be possible, seemed to unfold around her and she liked it.

"This is amazing," Cora grinned as she watched the children play.

"Amazing? That's tag," Remmy snorted. "Don't you get to play games inside the cities?"

"Games?" Cora repeated. "Um, well, I guess so, but not like this. We practice with virtual simulators that train us to be better citizens."

"Train you?" Remmy asked. "To do what?"

"Boring things, nothing really," Cora answered quickly. This was the first lie that Cora had ever told. The lie formed easily. She knew what she had just said was untrue, but somehow, she knew that telling Remmy the truth would have been worse. The simulators were really little more than virtual realms created by the ERC to desensitize the young citizens and train them to hate Emos. Cora must have killed hundreds, if not thousands, of digital Emos and thought nothing of it, but now she saw each one with Remmy's face and wanted to vomit.

"Sounds fun," Remmy quipped. "Anyway, you think Xander is going to be okay? He seems pretty angry for someone with an Em-Pak. I thought those things were supposed to make you zombies or something." He saw the look flash across Cora's face and quickly added, "No offense, of course."

"None taken," Cora smiled. "I think I was probably told some things about you that weren't true either."

"Sure seems like Xander believes them," Remmy added, looking back towards the tent.

"Xander believes whatever our father told him," Cora answered. "He wants nothing more than to join the ERC and become a politician, but can't stand the fact that our father wanted that for me."

"You didn't want it?" Remmy asked. "I mean, did you really have a choice? Couldn't they just *make* you?"

"No, it wasn't something that I wanted. That's for sure," Cora laughed. "And no, they couldn't make me. A lot of citizens are pretty brainwashed and they might like to blame their Em-Paks and the ERC, but the truth is that the Em-Paks only erase emotions once they show up. Most of the time you don't feel anything, then once in a while it'll beep, and then you go back to feeling nothing again. But in the end, we still make our own decisions. I just think that most citizens are too scared to make any decision that the ERC hasn't already made for them."

"You don't feel anything?" Remmy asked wide-eyed. "Nothing?"

"Pretty much," Cora admitted. "You can still feel, just not really anything more than okay though. At school, we'd whisper about emotions. You know, just rumors and stuff that we'd heard from older people who still remembered not having an Em-Pak."

"So you've never felt happy or sad or anything?" Remmy pressed on.

"No, I guess not," Cora answered. "But if you never did, then I guess you don't know what you're missing out on, right? Besides, none of us thought it was safe. We've all been told since birth that emotions lead to infection."

"But that's not true," Remmy protested, "why would they lie to you?"

"I can see that now," Cora nodded. "A lot of the stuff we were taught feels like lies now." Cora looked around the camp. Everything she had been taught felt like a lie.

"You shouldn't be afraid to feel things," Remmy said calmly. "Don't worry about not having the Em-Pak. Try not to get angry like you did back there with Xander, but other than that, you're safe to feel whatever you want."

"Really?" Cora asked hesitantly. "But what will I do if I feel that way again? Does that mean I'll turn into a Red?"

"No, not if you learn to control it," Remmy answered.

"That seems," Cora paused, she wanted to impossible, "difficult."

"Yeah, it can be," Remmy said honestly. "But you'll learn. I'll help   you."

With those simple words, Remmy calmed the turbulent waters that battered against Cora's mind. Things would be okay. Remmy would help her.

"Now, um, about those lies the ERC taught you," Remmy said slowly.

"Yes?" Cora asked. Her face scrunched with concern.

"Well, there's a pretty big one that we need to clear up," Remmy continued. "One that we kind of fed to the ERC, but we had to. You'll see."

"Um, okay?" Cora shrugged.

"It's the doctor," Remmy added, "the one who saved you and removed your Em-Pak."

"What about?" Cora asked.

Remmy stopped outside a large green canvas tent that was used as the hospital. He grabbed the large flap and pulled it aside for Cora to step inside. Bright lights were strung along the center support, illuminating the interior.

"See for yourself," Remmy motioned for Cora to go inside.

Cora hesitated and stepped in. Three rows of cots ran along each side and the strong tang of antiseptic filled the air. Various glass containers lined a small shelf, each filled with assorted medical supplies.

Cora cast a troubled look to Remmy, who stood behind her.

"It's okay," Remmy smiled, "really."

"Hello?" Cora asked as she stepped further into the tent.

"Cora?" a voice called from the back. It was gentle and tinged with wisdom. "Cora, wait right there. I'll be right out."

Cora's eyes went wide as the doctor emerged from around the back of a white screen.

"My lord, Cora, how you've grown," an old man smiled, his eyes wet with tears. "I never thought that I'd get to see you like this."

Samuel Eldritch, the first Samuel Eldritch, Cora's grandfather stood before her, but looked nothing like the imposing images of him produced by the ERC. This man seemed loving and gentle, nothing like her father and nothing like the shadow that she had been forced to live in.

"You're Samuel Eldritch?" Cora said hesitantly. "You're supposed to be dead."

"Yes," Samuel nodded, "it's me Cora. Please come in and sit. I'll explain everything. There is so much to tell you. So much for you to learn. I've missed you, Cora, missed you all dearly. I know it's all difficult for you to understand, but all will be made clear."

"You're supposed to be dead," Cora repeated and before she could stop herself, tears dotted her eyes as well.

-16-

Riots sprang up throughout the cities like mushrooms after the rain. The ERC demanded to know why Eldritch was allowing things to degenerate to their current levels, but he assured them that it was all part of the plan. Even though the ERC ultimately agreed, Eldritch could feel the noose tightening ever so slightly around his neck.

Eldritch looked over the program and codes created by his father. Each Em-Pak was individually coded for the implanted citizen. This made it easy for the ERC to track a malfunctioned or removed Em-Pak, but it also meant that Eldritch could zero in on individual Em-Paks, possibly amplifying their effects or completely turning them off. All he would need to do is gain access to the main server located inside the central ERC building in the Stele. This feat though, was far easier said than done.

The main server was located behind fourteen inch steel doors, security checkpoints and a myriad of other precautions that would prevent Eldritch from entering. The ERC Council themselves, hardly ever went into the main server room. So much careful planning and plotting had come down to this and all that separated Eldritch from realizing his aspirations were a few inches of steel.

The phone vibrated and danced across the papers scattered on Eldritch's desk, knocking a pen loose to roll to the floor. Eldritch momentarily reached for the pen, deeming it more important, but seeing that it was Captain Ortiz calling, stopped and snatched up the phone.

"Yes?" Eldritch answered, his Em-Pak beeping with each heartbeat.

"Sir?" Ortiz asked, "Are we on a secure line?" Ortiz was all business and Eldritch admired that. He had known that Ortiz was the right man for the job.

Eldritch paused and checked the small jamming unit sitting on the edge of his desk. The row of five small lights flashed bright green, signaling their fulfillment of purpose.

"Yes," Eldritch responded, "we're on a secure line. What is there to report, Captain?"

"Following riots, the Reds are continuing to crop up in small pockets throughout the outer cities," Ortiz began. "There have been some reports of minor outbreaks in some of the more secure cities. I don't think it will be long before there are Reds in the Stele. Perhaps, we need to expedite our plans, sir? The situation may become unmanageable soon."

"Agreed," Eldritch said. "The only remaining component to the realization of our plan is to gain access to the main server."

"The one within the central ERC building, sir?" Ortiz said slowly. His Em-Pak chirped a few times before the tension in his voice eased. Ortiz was a soldier, knew how to calculate battle risk and what Eldritch was asking seemed impossible. "I'm not exactly sure how that could be accomplished, sir."

"Just continue with the Emo insurgency," Eldritch barked. "As the Reds get closer to the Stele, make sure that you're not far behind. By my estimation, the infection and Reds should be within the walls by the end of the week. I want that building under siege."

"Under siege?" Ortiz questioned. "But sir, if the building is under attack, won't they lock it down and implement emergency protocol? Won't that make things more difficult?"

"Yes, they will, Captain, and that is exactly what I'm counting on. When the Council activates emergency procedures, the first action they will take is to address the citizens," Eldritch answered.

"Still sir, with all due respect, I don't see this adding up," Ortiz protested. The math of this plan was not balanced. Ortiz was a man that relied upon cold logic and statistics with or without an Em-Pak. "The employment of emergency protocols will make things incredibly difficult, sir."

"Not, if I'm inside when it happens," Eldritch said, his voice smooth and confident. "Like I said, you worry about playing up the Emo threat and I'll take care of the rest."

"Understood sir," Ortiz snapped.

"Good man," Eldritch responded and hung up.

Eldritch paused for a moment to consider what he had just ordered Captain Ortiz to do, but without an emotional frame of reference, all that could be understood was that each dead citizen would help pave the way to a better future. Surely, they would willingly offer up their lives, secure in the knowledge that their deaths were insignificant compared to the greater good. Beyond that, it really was nothing more than simple math, basic numbers and computation. Some citizens needed to die so that Eldritch could save the rest. The majority's needs out weighed the minority's rights. That was nature and there was no need to look beyond that explanation. He would save them from the ERC and their antiquated plan. The citizens deserved better leadership. They deserved Eldritch and had from the beginning, but the ERC Council had denied him his rightful place, his birthright. Soon they would learn the price for this slight.

Pressing a few keys on his computer, Eldritch called up the Em-Pak database. Countless, randomly sequenced numbers filled the spreadsheet on his screen. Regular citizens would never have had access to these numbers, would never have known the true identities of the ERC Council, but Eldritch was far from a regular citizen.

-17-

The funeral for Cora's mother was brief, but left an indelible mark upon her. She had been to other funerals, ones sanctioned and organized by the ERC to commemorate some supposed hero in the war against the Reds and Emos. But these had all been one dimensional, filled with no sense of loss or permanence. The politicians and ERC were simply cogs spinning in a massive machine. When one died, it was just replaced with another and things continued as if nothing had happened at all.

Unsanctioned funerals for family and friends had been outlawed by the ERC. These ceremonies, once a source of catharsis and comfort, were now deemed dangerous and unnecessary. Citizens were taught to forget the dead. Only those that had contributed to the cause were worth remembering. Besides, with the assistance and influence of an Em-Pak, Cora had never found the means, let alone the need to mourn anyone.

Now as Cora gazed in the narrow rectangular hole crudely scratched into the earth, she was overwhelmed by the surge of emotions. A crushing sense of loss weighed upon her. Numerous questions that could never be answered demanded to be voiced, but Cora kept her mouth closed, her teeth grinding together as silent tears rolled down her cheeks.

"So much sentimentality," Xander said, a note of disgust briefly flavoring his words. "It's just life, just science. If you're born, you're going to have to die. You're such a child sometimes, Cora. But I guess I should expect that from an Emo." Xander's Em-Pak chirped and he stopped talking, but his words had already cut Cora.

"She was our mother, Xander," Cora growled through gritted teeth. "That means something."

"If you say so," Xander shrugged as he kicked a clod of dirt into the open grave.

"Stop that!" Cora cried.

"What? This?" Xander asked as he kicked more dirt. "It's going to have to get filled in at some point. Otherwise the animals will come and –"

Cora's hand moved in a flash, leaving a bright red imprint of itself on Xander's cheek. The boy looked shocked for a moment and then seemed simply to absorb the pain.

"You done?" Xander smiled sickly as he gently touched his cheek.

"Yeah," Cora snapped. Her stomach felt like it was doing back flips and her head swam with anger as she glared at her brother. "Leave, Xander."

"I thought this was supposed to mean something, Cora?" Xander mocked. "Aren't I supposed to sit beside this hole in the dirt and think longingly of all of the wonderful times we *never* had with our mother. To fondly remember all of those times that *never existed?*"

"Xander," Cora said, a note of danger in her voice, "leave. Now." Her brother shrugged once more, kicked some more dirt, and turned to leave.

Cora collapsed to the ground, a sob erupting from her lips. Xander was an awful person, probably even without his Em-Pak, but he was right about one thing – there really were no good times to mourn. Cora had lived her entire life with a mother who was harnessed to an Em-Pak, so developing an emotional attachment to the woman had been nearly impossible. Some part of Cora though, knew that Xander was wrong.

The role of mother was something important, sacred even, and the loss of one was an event to mourn. Cora had never been given the chance to love her mother or to feel her mother's love, but she couldn't help but wonder if it was really there, buried deep underneath her Em-Pak. What if her mother never had an Em-Pak or had it removed? Would things have been different? Would she have been different? Cora believed that she would have been. She had to believe that the woman who had given her life would have loved her and silently hated her brother for mocking such a sacrosanct role.

"You okay?" Remmy's voice asked gently as he knelt down beside Cora. The other Emos allowed Cora alone time to mourn as she saw fit, but Remmy remained on the edge of the clearing just in case Cora needed him. "Kind of a stupid question to ask at times like these, but I mean are you as okay as you can be considering everything?"

"I guess," Cora sniffed. "Xander is such a jerk."

"I'd probably use a different word," Remmy grinned, "but he's your brother, so we'll stick with jerk for now."

"I wish Samuel could be here," Cora admitted. Her grandfather had wanted to be there, had even helped Remmy and his father dig the grave during the night, but couldn't be there with Cora, not with Xander around. It was simply too risky. Xander would surely recognize Samuel as his grandfather and no one could predict how he would react.

"I know," Remmy said as he placed a hand on Cora's shoulder. "I'm sure that he wishes that he could too, but with Xander, it would be too dangerous."

"Yeah," Cora mumbled, "I know." Her eyes traveled over to where Remmy's hand rested on her shoulder. It was a simple gesture, just the placement of a hand, really nothing more, but it somehow meant the world to Cora in that moment. It anchored her to the people that were still here, those that she could still care for and who could still care for her. "Thanks, Remmy."

"For what?" Remmy asked.

"I don't know," Cora shrugged, "everything, I guess."

"Already told you that you don't have to thank me," Remmy smiled.

He was so kind, so gentle. Why couldn't Xander be more like him, Cora wondered? Maybe no one could? Maybe there was only one person like Remmy in the entire world? And right now that person, that singularly amazing special person was right there with her.

Cora leaned into Remmy. He slowly wrapped his arm around her and tucked her head under his chin. No more words needed to be spoken. Nothing was left to say. Cora, feeling Remmy's support and strength, finally let go, and allowed herself to cry.

What she felt was terrible, like someone ripping her heart into shreds. She momentarily wondered if her pain and sadness were actually causing some sort of unseen physical harm.

"It's okay," Remmy said softly, "let it go. It's the only way to feel better."

Cora hated her Em-Pak. Hated that it had robbed her of her mother's love and of so much more, but these feelings were almost unbearable. How could a person survive them, let alone ever feel happy again? It seemed impossible. But with no other point of reference, Cora listened to Remmy's strong, steady voice. *Just let go...*

Tears blurred Cora's vision and stung her eyes. Remmy pulled his arm tighter. He said nothing, but continued to hold Cora as she cried beside her mother's grave.

In that moment, Remmy was the only thing that Cora could still believe in, could still think would ever put a smile on her face again. He was all that was real and right in the world. Slowly, she wrapped her arms around his waist and pulled him closer to her. It was strange to hug Remmy, something that Cora worried she might do wrong, but her arms seemed to fit perfectly around Remmy and his around her.

Cora had no idea how long she cried against Remmy, but he never faltered, remained steadfast the entire time. Remmy would always be there. Cora could feel that much.

-18-

The headquarters of the ERC Council, gray and imposing, looked even more so now that rings of sandbags and barbed wire surrounded it. The riots and Reds had finally reached the Stele and Eldritch couldn't have been more pleased. He imagined that without his Em-Pak, he would feel quite happy right now, very proud of himself and his careful planning.

"Are you sure this is a good idea, sir?" Captain Ortiz asked. Both he and Eldritch's aide rode in the back of his limo, their Em-Paks beeping with increased frequency as they approached the ERC Council building.

"Yes, of course it is," Eldritch nodded with confidence. There was no point second-guessing the plan now. Things had already reached a tipping point and he was unable to turn back.

"Sir?" the aide said as he held out a small flash drive. Eldritch had loaded it with the required override programs and Em-Pak ID numbers. All he had to do now was gain access to the main server.

"Thank you," Eldritch smiled. He propped his left shoe on his knee and twisted the heel, revealing a small compartment. Ortiz had designed it and lined it with a thin sheet of lead, ensuring that whatever was inside would remain invisible to the x-ray machines that waited at the doors on the ERC Council building. Dropping the flash drive inside the secret compartment, Eldritch twisted the heel and locked it back into place.

"Sir, you may want this as well," Ortiz held out an odd looking rectangular piece of plastic. Left in his briefcase, it would easily be overlooked as a random bit of office junk.

"And you're sure this works?" Eldritch asked as he looked at the plastic box.

"Absolutely sir," Ortiz nodded. "I tested it myself yesterday on a Red. Just twist the rear section. That will puncture the compressed air cartridge and fire the plastic projectiles. You get two shots from this weapon, Mr. Eldritch, so you'll need to make them count, sir. I'd recommend you aim for the face or neck, sir. The bullets may not be able to puncture body armor, but will definitely deliver a kill shot when fired at flesh, so avoid a chest shot and aim for *softer* targets."

"Outstanding, Captain," Eldritch beamed.

The limo rolled to a stop outside the ERC Council building. A group of ERC officers immediately surrounded the vehicle in a defensive circle and quickly whisked Eldritch out of the limo and into the building.

Dropping his briefcase and shoes onto a conveyor belt that fed the x-ray machine, Eldritch couldn't help but notice that his Em-Pak was chirping away like an over caffeinated sparrow. The guard on duty appeared to notice as well.

"Everything okay, Mr. Eldritch, sir?" the guard asked as the assemblyman's belongings were put into the machine.

"Okay?" Eldritch snapped. "Are you seriously that ignorant? No, everything is most certainly not okay, you moron. There are Reds within our city walls, the virus has resurfaced and the Emos have stepped up their terroristic activities. So no, you jackass, it is not okay!" It was risky to call the guard's bluff. But Eldritch was not known for his tolerance of underlings and he couldn't let on that he was here to overthrow the ERC.

"S-s-sorry, sir," the guard stuttered, holding his hands up in apology, his own Em-Pak beeping now. "I just meant that…I mean that I…"

"You meant what?" Eldritch growled. "That I should waste what precious little time I have to save our citizens and everything we hold dear to tolerate your asinine line of questioning? I should have you transferred to one of the outer cities so you can see firsthand just exactly how not okay things are."

"No sir. I mean, yes sir. I mean…" the guard tripped over his own words. "My sincerest apologies, Assemblyman Eldritch. I was completely out of line, sir. Please forgive my ignorance."

Eldritch took a deep breath and exhaled slowly, as if considering the guard's request. "Yes, of course. Just doing your job, right? No fault in that, I guess."

"Yes sir. Yes sir. Thank you, sir." the guard answered quickly as he handed Eldritch his shoes and briefcase, never once having looked at the x-ray machine's viewing screen.

"Good man," Eldritch smiled as he patted the guard on the shoulder. "You're right to be cautious. That's what you're here to do. Never know who can be trusted these days."

"Right you are, sir," the guard nodded. "Thank you, sir."

Eldritch slipped back into his shoes and began walking towards the elevator. Thus far, his plan had gone amazingly well.

The days in the Emo camp were peaceful and calm. Cora spent more and more time with her grandfather, Samuel, who was nothing like the stoic, cold visage she had been taught to worship by her father. Samuel was everything that her father wasn't and Cora found it difficult to comprehend the connection between the two.

"I just don't understand how you could be his father," Cora said. "How can my father be your son? It just doesn't make sense."

"Cora," Samuel said fondly, a warm smile on his face, "life is never so simple. It's never that black and white. I thought that it was, when I was younger and foolish. That line of thinking is what led me to create Em-Paks. It seemed logical at the time that if emotions were causing the virus, removing emotions would keep people safe. But we didn't understand enough and made a rash decision. People wanted an immediate solution, one that they wouldn't have to work for. The Em-Paks worked, but I never intended them to be a permanent solution."

"But then why do we still use them?" Cora questioned. She had spent many days in the hospital tent relentlessly questioning her grandfather. Any other free time was spent with Remmy learning to control her emotions or exploring the woods.

"Because the ERC saw them as a means to control people," Samuel said, his face darkened and aged with sadness. "I don't know, maybe I should have seen that someone would, but I just wanted to save people, to keep them safe from the Reds."

"Didn't you say anything?" Cora pressed on.

"Of course," Samuel smiled, but all the usual glee in his expression had vanished. "Even with an Em-Pak, I could understand the logical argument for slowly weaning the citizens from their Em-Paks. I reported my findings directly to the ERC Council."

"And?" Cora asked.

"And that's when they banished me from the Stele, from all cities actually," Samuel answered. "I escaped before the ERC could silence me permanently. Of course, they couldn't allow the citizens to know that, so they made it look like Reds attacked my car. Some poor soul was torn apart and buried in my coffin, but it wasn't me. They made my death a spectacle and used it to further their agendas. The ERC assumed because I was outside of the city walls that I was as good as dead. They never counted on me surviving. Once I was outside the walls, I quickly realized that my Em-Pak was going to make my survival much harder because it took away my fear. It prevented my natural instincts, those feelings and senses that have allowed us to climb as far as we have on the evolutionary ladder. Fear is what kept me alive at first, kept me away from the Reds. So I worked out the method to remove my Em-Pak and then began leaking word into the cities about how it could be done."

"Did my father know?" Cora asked. "I mean about your death? About the ERC and the Em-Paks? He must know now, right?"

"I'm not sure if he does and that he'd care if he did," Samuel said honestly. "I've kept tabs on him, on all of you, gleaning what small bits of information I could from newly arrived Emos and hacked ERC computer terminals. What I have pieced together about my son chills my soul. But I'm not sure how much I can really blame him. The ERC has groomed him, fostered the monster that he has become. He was young and just starting a family. I thought about taking him with me, but I didn't want to put any of you in danger. If your father vanished, the ERC would have known something was wrong. Then the rest of you would be in danger."

"Yes," Cora said coldly, "I can see how the ERC groomed Father. He was doing the same thing with me and Xander."

"I know," Samuel nodded, "but from what I hear, you weren't really cut out for the political spotlight."

Cora felt herself blush, those familiar waves of prickly heat now having a name and explanation. "I guess not. I just never really felt like doing what my father wanted me to do. Xander is a different story. Are you sure I can't tell him about you?"

"I wish we could," Samuel said, a note of true remorse tingeing his words. "But it's too risky. Xander is still harnessed to his Em-Pak, so there's no telling what his response might be. It could cause his Em-Pak to malfunction and then infection wouldn't be too far behind. It's just too risky I'm afraid."

"Don't you think you could convince him to have his removed?" Cora almost pleaded. She was thankful to have more than her grandfather's image influencing her life, and even more so now that she knew he was the opposite of everything that she had been taught, but this also made her feel an emptiness, a hole where the rest of her family should be. "Couldn't Xander be made to see the truth as well?"

"I wish I could say," Samuel answered. "But there really is no way to tell. From what you've told me, it seems that Xander is well indoctrinated by your father and the ERC. If we take his Em-Pak off, he may still react poorly and this sudden rush of emotions could kill him. Cora, it almost killed you."

Cora remembered the day of the crash. Walking through the woods with Remmy as he carried Xander and suddenly feeling a turbulent rush of what she now knew to be emotions flooding her body. She had believed that she was injured from the accident or maybe sick. Samuel had told her that having her Em-Pak damaged during the crash caused it to work erratically and nearly overwhelmed her body. People needed to be weaned from their Em-Paks. Cora's had just suddenly stopped working. Had Remmy not brought her to help as soon as he had, and Samuel not removed Cora's Em-Pak, she would have suffered a massive heart attack from the strain and died. Even if she had somehow survived the heart attack, she would have become a Red.

"But mine was broken," Cora protested. She had to believe that someone good was buried inside Xander, beneath his Em-Pak.

"That is true," Samuel nodded. "But all people who remove their Em-Paks run the risk of being overwhelmed by their emotions and suffering a heart attack or infection. With Xander being in the mindset that he is, it's simply too risky. It almost certainly would kill him. I'm sorry, dear, but we can't take that risk. We can't make that choice for him."

"I guess," Cora sighed. "I just thought maybe we could reach him, I don't know, find some way to make him see. I wish we could."

"Me too," Samuel admitted. "I know how difficult it can be to have your emotions back and not your family."

"Yeah," Cora said, but then tried to brighten the conversation. "But at least we've got each other, right? That's got to count for something."

"Very true," Samuel smiled as he mussed Cora's hair. "And you've evidently found yourself something else to count as well. Or should I say someone?"

"What are you talking about?" Cora asked, feeling the increasingly familiar prickly waves of heat dancing up and down her neck.

"Remmy?" Samuel asked, his voice full of mirth and eyebrows arched comically high.

"Remmy?" Cora repeated, her voice going high and thin. But she knew that Samuel was right, could feel it in her gut and more importantly, her heart. Something happened when Remmy was around. A strange and terrifying, yet completely addicting and enjoyable feeling warmed Cora, but she had yet to place a name to it. What she felt around Remmy was something that Cora had never known, but keenly missed when he wasn't around.

Samuel couldn't help himself and a deep, good-natured laugh rumbled up from his gut. "Yes, Remmy?"

"What?" Cora demanded, suddenly feeling a twinge of what Remmy had explained as anger. "Why do you keep saying Remmy's name?" Samuel's eyes darted over Cora's shoulder.

"Um, because I'm standing behind you," Remmy said, a slight smile curling the edges of his lips.

"How long have you been there?" Cora snapped, her entire body now awash in those increasingly familiar waves of prickly heat.

-20-

The elevator binged loudly and shuddered to a stop. Eldritch stepped out onto the floor of the main server. Two guards turned to face him, not used to having people step out of the elevator on their floor.

"Sir?" one of guards asked, his machine gun slightly raised. "With all due respect, Mr. Eldritch, I think you may have pushed the wrong button, sir."

Eldritch moved with purpose and sense of clarity that was only afforded by his Em-Pak. There were no nagging thoughts of self-doubt, no need to consider the morality of his plan. What he was doing was important, but beyond that, it was his nature. Why should he be made to feel bad for simply following that? Wasn't that his design?

With a quick half twist of the small plastic box, Eldritch watched a cloud of compressed air burst forward. The projectile moved with such speed that it was lost in the space between passing seconds. The approaching guard's head snapped back and he fell to the floor. A dark pool of blood began creeping across the polished floor.

The second guard fumbled for his gun, unsure of what was transpiring before him. His Em-Pak angrily chirped away as his hands tangled in the strap of the machine gun strung over his shoulder.

Eldritch gave the small box a second and final twist. A loud *puff* echoed through the hallway. The remaining guard's hands, still tangled, struggled to reach the small hole in the center of his neck. Blood pulsed from the injury, covering the front of his uniform. Eldritch couldn't help but think that it somewhat resembled a rather morbid necktie.

"Sorry gents," Eldritch said, free of remorse. Grabbing the guards' two keycards from around their necks, Eldritch slid them through the scanner in the correct sequence that very few people knew. The heavy metal door slid silently to the side revealing a large dark room.

The deafening whir of numerous fans attempting to keep the server room cool battered the sides of Eldritch's head. It was of no matter. He would be gone soon enough or had better be.

The main server towered above Eldritch's head, dominating the center of the room like some long forgotten obsidian obelisk. Small red and green lights danced on the sides. Locating the panel detailed in his father's notes, Eldritch twisted the release and silently dropped it to the floor. A small port surrounded by a series of multicolored twisting wires waited patiently within the tiny compartment. Eldritch lifted his shoe, released the false heel, and retrieved the flash drive.

Looking around one last time, Eldritch plunged the flash drive into the port and watched as the sequence of lights changed. Strange that something as small and seemingly harmless as the change of a light's color could signal what was about to come. The tiny flicker of an LED bulb harkening the beginning of a new era, one helmed by Eldritch.

Grabbing the guards, Eldritch dragged them one at a time into the sever room. Someone would probably notice that they weren't at their posts and would definitely notice the wide streaks of blood painted across the floor, but that wouldn't matter soon.

Eldritch casually stepped back into the elevator and smoothed the wrinkles in his suit. He needed to look good for his television appearance. The members of the ERC Council, Eldritch mused as his Em-Pak tried valiantly to erase his smug sense of satisfaction, well that was a different story altogether.

-21-

Ripples, like liquid glass, gently moved the pine needle through the current in lazy circles. Cora found it mesmerizing. She had never known what free time felt like or could be used for. Days behind the city walls were spent preparing, studying ERC laws and politics. Never had there been time, let alone hours, just to enjoy being alive. Cora had come to realize that she had never actually enjoyed anything before the accident. Now all that was changing. Cora was changing.

A small waterfall cascaded at the far end of the pool, throwing a light mist into the air that kissed Cora's cheeks. The waterfall roared as it crashed against the jagged rocks below, adding to the hypnotic nature of the setting. Sights like these didn't exist inside the cities, would have been outlawed and Cora could understand why. Sitting here, lost in nature, Cora found herself sorting through a deep well of long suppressed feelings and thoughts. Many of them were about her mother, father, and Xander. More were about Remmy.

"It's hard to look away, right?" Remmy grinned as he plopped down into the grass beside her. He began toying with a stick, drawing small designs in the dirt.

"Huh?" Cora muttered, lost in her own thoughts.

"The pine needle," Remmy answered. "You never think to look at something like that, but then you do and you can't look away."

"Yeah," Cora nodded, joining the conversation. She leaned back on her elbows, enjoying the sensation of the soft grass against her skin. "I'm not even sure how long I've been looking at it."

"Yup," Remmy smirked, "that's how it goes. I love being out here, away from camp, from everyone."

"Antisocial much?" Cora laughed. "I'll leave you with your thoughts then." She faked getting up, but Remmy's hand shot out and grabbed her elbow.

"I was going to say, I felt that way before you showed up," Remmy smiled, his eyes seemed unable to meet Cora's. "I like sharing this with you. I like you, Cora."

"I like you too, Remmy," Cora said, not understanding Remmy's point. Having never had emotions, Cora lacked awkward conversation practice. "I mean you're weird and have a totally strange name, but I still like you." The smile on Cora's face held no notes of insult, rather it reached deep into Remmy's chest and gently plucked the strings of his heart.

"Hey! I'm named after a famous artist," Remmy smirked. "It's completely a reasonable name." He smiled back, unknowingly having the same effect upon Cora.

"You're talking to someone who lived in the city with an Em-Pak, remember? No art, no music," Cora grinned. "So sorry, but your name is still strange."

Forgetting about the name debate, Remmy tried to clarify his earlier point, "I mean that I *like* you, Cora. Like more than anyone else."

"You like the word like too," Cora teased. "Do all boys talk this way?"

"What way?" Remmy asked.

"With tons and tons of words, but never really saying anything," Cora grinned.

"I dunno," Remmy said, suddenly looking crestfallen.

"What's wrong?" Cora asked, worried she had teased Remmy too much. "I'm sorry if I – Remmy, I didn't mean to…"

"No it's not that," Remmy said, staring at the ground.

"Then what is it?" Cora asked gently. "What's wrong?"

"Nothing," Remmy grunted.

"Remmy," Cora said as she softly brushed his arm. She had no idea why she had reached out to touch him. It's not like she needed to get his attention because she had that. And it's not like she needed to touch him, but she did, some part of her needed to. In that moment, when Remmy looked so sad, Cora needed to touch him, to comfort him.

Remmy lifted his head to say something to Cora, to mutter some words, but as he met her eyes, the words suddenly became stuck in his throat. He leaned forward, silently praying that Cora would do the same or at least not pull away from him.

The sound of her heartbeat filled Cora's ears. She couldn't hear Remmy, though it didn't look like he was saying anything. He was simply leaning towards her slowly, his eyes locked on hers. Cora found herself unable to do anything other than the same. As Remmy's lips softly brushed Cora's, her heart threatened to explode. Part of Cora was terrified by these new feelings, but that part was kept at bay by the one that reveled in them.

Raising his hand, Remmy ran his fingers through Cora's hair. It was cool and smooth, the perfect complement to the soft warmth of her lips. Everything about Cora was perfect.

"Remmy," Cora whispered as she rested her head against his. "I like you too."

"Good," Remmy smiled. He didn't know what else to say. There was nothing else to say.

"Can we try that again?" Cora asked, a note of mischief in her voice.

"Yes," Remmy said faster than he had intended. "I mean, yeah, sure." *Smooth*, he silently mocked himself. He needed to get it together. Couldn't blow it with Cora.

The two leaned forward, their lips gently brushing each other's once again. Things seemed to slow, with their volume turned down. All that there was in that moment was Remmy and Cora joined by a soft, innocent kiss.

A feral scream shattered the fragile silence, shaking the two kissers from their sweet, stolen moment.

A second scream. Then a third. Soon it was too many to count.

"Cora," Remmy gasped, leaping to his feet, pulling her up with him, "we have to run. We have to run now!"

-22-

The inner chamber of the ERC Council, once quiet and ominous, was now a buzzing mass of cameras and lights, all in preparation for the Council to address the citizenry. Things had gone far enough, they told Eldritch. It was time to reclaim order and get the citizens back in line.

How right you are, Eldritch thought, as he saw the shadowy figures of the ERC Council file into their chamber and take their assigned places. These people thought they were safe, hidden by shadows and fear, but Eldritch knew better. The Council was made of people just like him, like everyone else. They were no different from the citizens they controlled, who relied on Em-Paks to keep them safe. And just like those people without an Em-Pak, were just as vulnerable to infection as the rest of the citizens.

Eldritch smiled as he fingers brushed the small trigger device in his coat pocket now linked to the main server. His Em-Pak beeped and he quickly moved his thoughts elsewhere, not wanting to draw attention or suspicion.

The camera crew took their places and began to countdown. Everyone fell silent within the ERC Council's Chamber, not wanting to interrupt such an important address and fearful of the consequences if they did.

"Citizens," one of the ERC Council members began, "we have lived for many years secure in the knowledge that we were safe. Protected from the virus by our Em-Paks and protected from the Reds and Emos through the tireless efforts of the ERC, but our situation has changed. It has evolved and become even more dangerous. The Emos, once thought to be nothing more than misguided dreamers, have finally shown their true colors. They are terrorists, single minded in their desire to undermine and destroy everything that we have worked for, everything that we hold dear. Now, the Reds have joined the Emos in their mission of terror. This new threat must be eradicated, excised, and destroyed like the cancer it is. Rest assured in the knowledge that the ERC will protect you. The ERC will usher you safely through these troubling times and into an era of calm and control."

Eldritch had waited for this moment. The ERC Council had made its grand promise and now Eldritch would expose just how empty it was. Slipping his hand into his coat pocket, Eldritch pushed the small red button in the center of the trigger device. Nothing happened. He waited and still nothing happened. Had he put in the proper codes? Of course, he had. He had double and triple checked them. Was it the device? Maybe his father's notes had been wrong, but how was that possible? He had designed the Em-Pak. If anyone's notes were correct, they were his, but still nothing happened.

"We are here to serve you, the citizens," the ERC Council continued. There was more to the speech, Eldritch had read it himself, but the Council member stopped. Had they lost their place? That seemed unlikely.

Two of the shadowy figures of the ERC Council rose from their seats and turned to face the one delivering the speech. Were they going to take over? The dark outlines of their heads whipped back, arms spread wide as a terrifying scream erupted from their mouths.

The Council member at the podium turned to face the two flanking them from the sides.

"My God," the ERC Council member cried. "Someone help us! Help us please!" Fear was present in those words, real fear. The kind felt without an Em-Pak.

Eldritch watched the ERC Council being torn apart by its own members. Those that were infected ripped into the others with wanton abandon. One member, yet to be infected, but whimpering in fear, tried to crawl away. Her face became partially visible as she scrambled out from under the large table at which she had previously sat. Hands with fingers curled and bloody, darted out from under the table, clamping around the woman's legs, attempting to drag her back under the table. All broadcast for the citizens to see.

"Eldritch! Eldritch, please!" she cried.

The hammering of heavy boots on the floor filled the room. Eldritch refused to move, refused to help. Anyone in the room who showed any signs of being infected or appeared at risk for infection was about to be sanitized.

The woman cried out one more time. A final weak whine before a tangled mass of bloodied hands shot out from under the table, joining the first set and dragged her underneath. Her cries for help were cut short by a wet choke and sickening snap. A large dark pool crept from underneath the table.

"What are you waiting for?" Eldritch barked at the nearest ERC officer. "Get this under control immediately." With the ERC Council in pieces and covered in its own blood, Eldritch was the next highest official in the room.

Waves of gunfire erupted in the room, chewing the long, semi-circular table, once a symbol of the ERC Council's power and status, to pieces. One member, infected and protected behind the table, leapt onto the top. The member's eyes were wild as he crouched on the table, a feral expression carved into his wrinkled face.

Eldritch watched with satisfaction as the ERC Council member launched himself from the top of the table, his fingers curled into gore-caked claws. Bullets tore into the man, dropping him to the floor in a tangled heap.

"Clear!" a young ERC officer called as he was swept behind and under the table.

"Sir?" another officer asked, gently grabbing Eldritch's elbow.

"What?" Eldritch snapped.

"Sir, the cameras were still on," the ERC officer continued. "I'm not sure whether or not the feed was cut. We're looking into it now."

"Forget it," Eldritch waved as he walked towards the ruined ERC Council table.

"Sir?" the officer questioned.

"Are the cameras on?" Eldritch snapped at the nearest cameraman. "Make sure the feed is streaming live to all cities. Make sure all citizens see this." He waved at the carnage that surrounded him.

The cameraman waved his arms trying to gain Eldritch's attention, "Assemblyman Eldritch, sir, the feed was never cut. We're live right now, sir."

"Good," Eldritch nodded with a reptilian grin. He walked behind the blood stained and bullet chewed podium at the center of the ERC Council table. Turning towards the camera, Eldritch straightened his tie and smoothed his suit. "Citizens," Eldritch said slowly, "you are no doubt as troubled as I am over what has just transpired. To see the ERC Council, once trusted with protecting you, tearing itself apart, infected by the very thing they were tasked with eradicating. And without question, you, like myself, would like to know why. Why has the ERC Council failed you so miserably? What could have been done differently? What does this mean for the rest of us? For our very way of life?" Eldritch paused to allow his questions to sink in. He walked slowly past the ruined, mangled bodies of the ERC Council, motioning to the battered remains strewn before him. The camera captured it all.

"Sadly, citizens," Eldritch continued, "this could have all been avoided. I recently discovered notes from my father detailing a needed upgrade to the main Em-Pak server. The Council knew of this for years, but kept the information suppressed for reasons that even I struggle to comprehend. Perhaps they were worried that a momentary shutdown of the server would result in a loss of control. Maybe they were right, but I saw an opportunity in the chaos that swelled throughout our cities. In that time, when we were distracted, I moved to fix the server, upgrade our Em-Pak programming and save us all. I was, admittedly, too late with regards to the members of the ERC Council, or perhaps they had moved their devices to another server. I believe that the Council sought methods to save themselves, not the citizenry, and I say that they have reaped the twisted, deceitful fruit from the seeds they have sown. Rest assured, citizens, that I am still here to serve you. I, like my father, am constant in my mission to keep you safe, to end your suffering. I will take back control and reinstate order; you have my word. The ERC Council has failed because they forgot who they serve, forgot that they too were citizens. I will not. I will serve you, as one of you, as it should have been from the beginning. The Council is no more, but the ERC remains. I remain and so shall you."

Eldritch moved from the camera's view. As soon as he was sure that it was off, he pulled his phone from his pocket. "Ortiz?" Eldritch said quietly. "Pull them back. Clear the cities. Regroup with the rest of the ERC forces and clear the infected. We are in total control."

-23-

The Reds stood atop the waterfall screaming with primal ferocity. Cora could count at least seven and saw movement in the surrounding woods. They were closing in on her and Remmy.

"Cora, you need to listen to me," Remmy said, his eyes wide and panicked. "We're going to run, but if we have to fight, don't let yourself get too angry. Keep breathing. Remember, in through your nose, out through your mouth. Think about the pine needle. Think about something calming. Don't get angry, okay?" Fear of losing Cora was superseded by the fear of her becoming infected, becoming a Red.

"Okay. Okay," Cora said quickly as she grabbed Remmy's arm and began moving away from the stream. The truth was that Cora was barely listening to Remmy's words and definitely was not thinking about the pine needle twirling gently on the currents. All she could think about was running, getting away from the Reds. Panic wound itself around her heart, shortening her breath and making her head swim. Cora's vision began to narrow to a pinpoint.

"Breathe!" Remmy shouted as he took the lead and pulled Cora along behind him. "Keep breathing! Just keep breathing!"

"I'm trying!" Cora gasped. "Can't we just climb a tree?"

"No time," Remmy wheezed. "They'd grab us before we got high enough. Just keep moving."

The Reds were close behind. Ten of them spilled out of the woods and onto the narrow path. They moved as a pack. The Red in the lead, a large man holding a short axe, set the pace for the others. They were all smeared with dirt, hair hanging in large, tangled knots. Bright red paint streaked across their faces and bodies. At least, Cora hoped it was paint.

Remmy had screwed up, could feel it in his bones. How had he been so careless with Cora? Why had he taken her somewhere that was so far from the camp and the watch? But Remmy knew why. He wanted to be alone with Cora, to have her to himself, away from Xander, away from the others. But this greed now threatened to end both their lives. Remmy would do whatever he had to keep Cora safe.

"Cora, run for the camp!" Remmy shouted. "No matter what, don't stop. Get to the camp!"

"What about you?" Cora panted as she pushed her legs to move faster and faster.

Remmy grunted something that sounded like 'slow them down' and skidded to a halt. Cora stumbled, realizing that Remmy had stopped. She turned to go back, but the look in Remmy's eyes stopped her.

"GO!" Remmy yelled as he grabbed a heavy rock from the ground. "Cora, go!"

Cora's vision blurred as tears welled in her eyes. She ran faster. Remmy was going to take on an entire pack of Reds with only a rock. He was going to die and it was all her fault. Why had she let him lead her so far from the safety of the camp? Why had she been so selfish?

"Help! Help!" Cora screamed even though her lungs felt like they would burst at any moment. "Reds! Help!" She prayed that someone would hear her.

Remmy steadied his legs and prepared to fight. Every fiber in his being screamed for him to run and get as far from the Reds as he could, but he had to buy Cora time, and he had to keep her safe, no matter what.

As the Reds closed in on Remmy, he was shocked to find that his thoughts were not on living, dying, or even fighting. All he could think of was that stolen moment with Cora and that soft kiss, the feel of her lips gently brushing against his, the feel of her hair between his fingers. Cora was the last thing he would think of before he left this earth. Whatever was going to happen, Remmy was determined that Cora would be the last thing he would think about. He would die with love in his heart, not fear.

The lead Red raised his axe as he came close to Remmy, his eyes narrowed and angry. Remmy could see strings of thick saliva strung between the Red's yellowed, pointed teeth as he screamed.

Pointed teeth? The thought flashed through his mind. No one had ever spoken about the Reds having fangs. Granted, Remmy had never cared to look, but he couldn't help but feel something was missing from everyone's understanding of the Reds.

Waiting a few more seconds, a few more heartbeats, Remmy pulled back and fired the stone directly into the face of the approaching Red. The rock collided with the Red's nose with a hollow *thunk*, collapsing him to the ground. Remmy ran forward, shocking the other Reds and causing them to hesitate long enough for him to deliver a vicious kick to the face of the downed leader before grabbing his axe. Remmy raised the axe.

"Come on!" Remmy snarled. "Come on!"

The Reds slowly circled Remmy, their own weapons raised and ready.

Remmy swung the axe with all of his force at the nearest Red, but three more fell on him from the sides. Remmy vanished underneath the savage attacks of the Reds.

-24-

Eldritch couldn't feel happy, but he imagined that he might, given what he had just accomplished. Why waste time with messy elections and politics when he could simply seize control? The ERC Council had stood in his way for far too long and now they were gone. It really had been the Council's own fault. Had they recognized his greatness, Eldritch never would have been forced to take control of the ERC in such a dramatic fashion. Then again, had the transition not been so theatrical, the citizens might not have fallen in line as beautifully as they had.

The days following the televised downfall of the ERC Council had been tenuous, the citizenry uneasy and difficult to control. Once they saw Captain Ortiz and the his ERC Special Forces sweep through the streets, clearing the cities of both Reds and 'Emos', the citizens fell in line. After all, like all sheep, they wanted the security and routine provided by a strong shepherd. Eldritch was more than happy to step into this role and provide that much sought after sense of order.

The cities were bruised, some buildings destroyed, a few fires lit, and of course, the countless dead, but these were just growing pains, nothing more really. Eldritch didn't have time to think about these things. He was tasked with the far more important business of setting things right. And the first place to do that was in the ERC Council room.

Eldritch had the room scrubbed, removed all the archaic furniture and overpowering lights. He was going to govern as a citizen, in plain view, protected of course by Captain Ortiz and his men.

"Mr. Eldritch, sir?" Captain Ortiz asked as he entered the room. The tang of cordite and disinfectant still hung heavy in the air, but new furniture had already been moved in. Eldritch sat behind a large, highly polished oak desk, which sat directly in front of a large, semi-circular window. It was odd that Eldritch had never even known the window existed, having been hidden away behind heavy black curtains that covered the walls. Ortiz had cautioned against sitting near such a large window, Eldritch making himself an easy target, but Eldritch insisted. The window provided him with the ability to survey his city, and more importantly, for his citizens to see him, and remember that he was always present in their lives, always watching.

"Is this about the window again, Captain?" Eldritch mumbled as he rifled through a stack of papers. "Because I thought that we had cleared all of that up with the installation of bullet proof glass? Or is there a problem with the Reds?" Eldritch would pretend to love his citizens, but he was a long way off from trusting them.

"No sir," Ortiz responded. "The window is acceptable now. We have reports of Reds moving on the outer edges of the cities, but they'll be sanitized soon."

"Then what is it, Captain?" Eldritch's Em-Pak chirped. He was growing impatient.

"There is still a small pocket of Council supporters holed up in one of the outer cities," Ortiz answered. "They have a very visible position, so I think it would be prudent to try to get them to surrender without a show of overwhelming force. A public execution might have some unwanted effects."

"Hmm, yes, I guess that would be best," Eldritch nodded. His transition to power had been relatively smooth, but some small bands of people still stupidly clung to the old ways of doing things, insisting on the creation of a new Council. But their refusal to accept Eldritch's authority would be their undoing as well. "No need for violence, Captain, at least not yet. Have we determined who this rebellious lot is composed of?"

"Some sir," Ortiz nodded. "We have them under surveillance. They don't appear to be making any major plans, not really doing more than barricading themselves in a small ERC office."

"Names, Captain," Eldritch grunted. He waved his hands impatiently.

"We have positively identified two people within the office," Ortiz answered. "One is a low level assistant named Brian Christopher and the other is Assemblywoman Toni Marsh."

"Marsh? Really?" Eldritch chuckled. "I didn't think that woman had the sand to do something like this. Shame really, she could have been useful." Eldritch moved to the computer atop his desk and began punching keys. "Perhaps, she will still be able to contribute to the cause."

"Anything further, sir?" Ortiz asked.

"No, I think we're good now, Captain," Eldritch said absently. "With Marsh and her aide's Em-Paks turned off, they'll take care of that little pocket of resistance for us. Just have your men on standby to clean it up."

"Understood," Ortiz grunted.

"Oh, and Captain," Eldritch looked up from his computer, "one more thing."

"Yes, sir?" Ortiz stopped at the door.

"No survivors," Eldritch stated coldly.

"Understood, sir," Ortiz saluted and left the office.

-25-

Cora led the others from the camp back towards where she and Remmy had been ambushed. Xander meandered down the trail beside her, not out of a sense of concern, but more out of boredom.

"This is what happens," Xander mumbled as he walked next to Cora. "I could have told you that this would happen. Nothing good is going to come from being outside the city walls."

Cora turned a fiery glare on her brother. "Are you serious? Right now, Xander? Of all times to be a jerk?" Cora snapped. "Remmy saved my life and all you can say is *I told you so*? Why the hell are you even here if you care so little?"

"What else am I supposed to do?" Xander shrugged. "I can't sit in that smelly tent all damn day. Looking for your little boyfriend at least gives me something to do for a while."

"Just go away," Cora barked. "I don't need your help. Remmy doesn't need your help."

"Whatever," Xander said flatly. He turned off the trail and began walking through the woods. "Remmy doesn't need anyone's help…because he's probably dead."

Cora ignored her brother's words. She was out here to find Remmy, not fight with Xander.

"Should we follow him?" one of the camp guards asked.

"No," Cora shook her head, "Xander is a lot of talk, but he's not stupid and won't go too far. He's got no idea how to survive out here alone and has no idea where he is."

"Okay," the guard said with more than a little concern. "Even so, maybe we shouldn't let him get too far out of sight."

"Good idea," Cora responded. "I just don't want someone who should be looking for Remmy to be wasting time babysitting my bratty little brother."

The rest of the walk was done in silence, everyone listening for Remmy, Reds, or both. The woods were silent, expect for their usual noises. How could birds sing at a time like this, Cora wondered? How could their songs sound so happy when things were so wrong? Hadn't the world noticed that Remmy was missing? These questions and countless others whipped through

Cora's insides like shards of glass caught in a windstorm. By the time she arrived at the spot, Remmy had made his stand. Cora felt as if her insides were little more than a tattered tangle of ribbon, the pieces of herself, only recently fit together, now frayed and torn apart.

A large dark spot covered the ground. Numerous sets of footprints circled the area. A rock, smeared with clotted blood sat discarded near the tangled bramble that edged the small clearing.

"Looks like the kid put up one hell of a fight," one of the other Emos said to Remmy's father. "I'm sorry."

Remmy's father tried to say something, anything, but the words, fragile and only partially formed broke apart and lodged themselves in his throat. A wet choking sound was all he seemed capable of producing. Remmy's father fell to his knees, his head on the ground and shoulders heaving as he sobbed.

Cora knelt down and touched the stain. The ground was still wet. She looked at her fingers, red and gritty. Was this the last memory she would have of Remmy? How could fate be so cruel to allow the memory of Remmy's kiss to be followed by something so terrible? How was this fair?

Three men helped Remmy's father from the ground and promised to keep looking for his boy, but right now, they thought it was best if he went back to the camp. They would stay out here all night if they needed to. Remmy's father nodded. As she walked past, the bloodshot eyes of Remmy's father momentarily met Cora's. His eyes were ringed in red and shot with veins. He suddenly looked frail, as if a sudden breeze might carry him away.

"I'm sorry," Cora said in little more than a whisper. She waited for Remmy's father to yell, blame her, and tell her that his son never would have been out here if not for her. This was her fault. She had killed Remmy. Cora waited but it never came.

"Don't," Remmy's father's voice cracked. Cora was unsure if he meant don't even try to apologize or don't even speak to him, but he continued. "Don't blame yourself, Cora."

"But I..." Cora's words pained her and refused to be spoken. "If I hadn't..." Tears began to stream down her cheeks.

Remmy's father pulled Cora into a hug. She tensed, unsure of what this meant, but relaxed as the man began to sob. "My son loved you. I could see that. Thank you for giving him that gift. Thank you, Cora."

"Remmy loved me?" Cora asked, her words trembling and voice cracking. In that moment, Cora realized that what she had felt near Remmy, holding his hand, kissing him, must have been love. That strange and terrifying, but completely addictive and wonderful rush of emotions was love. Remmy loved her. She loved him. Now, she would never be able to tell him.

Cora and Remmy's father walked back to the camp in silence.

-26-

A dull *thrum-thrum-thrum* radiated through Remmy's head in waves. His eyes were swollen, but he forced them to open to half slits. Had his entire body not been racked with pain, he would have believed that he was dead, but there was no way he was dead, not when he felt this awful.

Golden rays of sun filtered in through a rusted corrugated metal roof. Large motes of dust danced in the dappled sunlight, but Remmy shared none of their lightness or mirth. The Reds had taken him somewhere, but where? Why hadn't they killed him? Remmy pondered these questions, knowing that he was no closer to providing an answer than he was to getting out of this disgusting shack that served as his prison.

Willing the pain out of his head, Remmy tried to clear his thoughts and form some idea, some plan. There was very little in the shack. It was really nothing more than a small wooden square cobbled together out of discarded bits of wood, pallets mostly, and a rusted sheet of metal for the roof. No windows and one door left Remmy with very few options. The dirt floor was hard packed, but maybe he could dig his way under a wall. At least the Reds had left his arms and legs untied. They weren't expecting Remmy to escape.

Remmy cast glances into the murky corners of the shack. Three were empty. One held a rumpled pile of old clothes. Remmy figured someone had used it as bedding. His body screaming in protest, Remmy forced himself up from the dirt floor and shuffled over to inspect the tangled pile of rags. Maybe, just maybe, there was something he could use. Remmy grabbed the corner of what looked to have once been a large flannel shirt and tugged. The pile resisted for a second, as if it were glued to the floor, but then came loose with a sound of kindling tumbling to the floor.

"What the hell?" Remmy muttered. Why would there be a bunch of sticks wrapped in old clothes? His sore brain slowly pieced together the image displayed in front of him in the dim light. The clothes were stuck to the ground, a dried puddle of gore and bits of leathery flesh holding them in place. It was bones.

Remmy was holding the remains of the last occupant of his prison cell.

"Gross," Remmy gagged as he backed away from the remains.

The door of the shack shook as someone removed the lock and pulled the door open. It stuck, catching the jamb, but was yanked open with incredible force. Remmy was shocked to see a young girl standing in the doorway, framed in the golden hues of the day's dying sun.

"Sit down," the girl said, her voice sounded muddled, as if she had to struggle to force out the words.

Remmy thought about attacking her, making a run for it, but the Reds never would have allowed her in here unless others were outside. He might make it past the girl, but that would be it. His victory and life would both be short lived. Left with few other options, Remmy put his back against the wall and slid down onto the hard packed dirt floor.

"You're from the Emo camp in the woods, right? The one outside of the Stele?" the girl asked. Her words were a little more formed, as if she were regaining her ability to speak.

"I'm not telling you anything," Remmy snapped. Having a conversation with a Red was strange, but Remmy wasn't going to tell them anything. There was no way he was going to give the Reds even the slightest idea where his parents and Cora were. He'd die to protect them and figured he probably would have to.

"I'm not really asking," the girl chuckled. "The question was, um, what's the word?" She paused and then beamed, "Rhetorical! That's it! It was a rhetorical question." She took a few more steps into the shack. Remmy could see a collection of small, wicked looking blades hanging around her waist from a thick leather belt. Small skulls, some from animals, some from children, hung between the blades like trophies.

"Rhetorical?" Remmy laughed in spite of his fear. "That's a big word for a Red. Honestly, I'm amazed you can string together a sentence, let alone use dictionary words. I thought you Reds were supposed to be raving idiots. No offense, of course."

The girl let out a chortled laugh. Both her words and laughter sounded garbled, as if it formed in her throat, but was cut to pieces in her mouth. "Yes, well that is what we were taught to think, isn't?"

"How the hell do you know what I was taught, you troll?" Remmy growled. The fact that the Red used 'we' instead of 'you' sent acidic knots roiling through Remmy's stomach. The back of this throat burned and he struggled to swallow.

Another mangled string of laughter spilled from the girl's mouth. "Because I was taught it as well. Don't you remember sitting in class next to me? How we used to sneak off at our lunch break to go walk in the fields? Surely, you remember that, Remmy, don't you?"

Hearing his name caused the fear in Remmy's gut to blossom with malignant force, toxic vines twisted and wrapped around his innards. The disgusting shack appeared to shift, like a boat gently lolling on waves. "Who...who are you?" Remmy stuttered, but the answer was already pressing down upon him.

"Come on now, Remmy," the girl said slowly as she sat down across from him. "I know it's been a while, but you're going to tell me that you don't recognize your best friend, Jessica? I thought we were better friends than that, Remmy. Honestly, I think my feelings are a little hurt."

"Jessica?" Remmy asked. "How? Your family was killed. You were dead."

"Dead?" Jessica grinned, revealing savagely pointed teeth. "No, not exactly."

"But how?" Remmy asked, astonished that somewhere inside of this monster was his old friend. She was wild looking, covered in red markings and definitely dirtier than the last time he had seen her, but he couldn't deny that this was Jessica.

"We'll get to that," Jessica smiled. "In fact, you'll find out first hand."

"What happened to you? To your teeth?" Remmy asked, choosing to ignore Jessica's implied threat. He needed to grab whatever bits of information he could. Keeping Jessica talking was the only chance Remmy had.

"Beautiful, aren't they?" Jessica smiled as she tilted her head back, opened her mouth and ran her tongue along the wicked little daggers that filled her mouth.

Remmy fought the urge to gasp as he saw the extra row of pointed teeth in Jessica's mouth. Thoughts of the sharks he had seen in his schoolbooks filled Remmy's head. He figured that the connection probably wasn't too far off.

"Stare if you want to," Jessica grinned. "I know what you're thinking. I thought it too when I was first brought here. How could someone file their teeth to look like that? How could they bear the pain? But that's the best part, Remmy. You don't have to, it just happens after a while. Even better, you have an endless supply for the Tooth Fairy." Jessica laughed, she used the point of her knife to flick the extra row of teeth in her mouth. "One falls out and another pops into place. It's great."

"No, it's not," Remmy protested, "it's awful. Jessica, how could you let this happen to you?"

"Let it?" Jessica chuckled. "Remmy, it just happens. There's no more choice in this than there is your hair growing. It's natural. It's the evolution of the virus, of the Love Bug." Jessica paused to laugh again. "My God, remember when we used to call it that? Who would have guessed this is what it does to someone if they survive the first phase."

"First phase?" Remmy repeated. "What are you talking about?"

"The whole screaming crazy part," Jessica answered, "that's just the first phase of infection. We were wrong when we thought that was how the virus left someone. Problem was that most people were too crazy to survive that part, so no one ever saw what was next, but we've fixed that. And Remmy, let me tell you, if you survive the first part, it's amazing. Just imagine never being afraid. Never having to worry again."

"What do you mean, if I survive?" Remmy spat. "I'm not like you. I'll never be like that."

"Your choice," Jessica shrugged as she got up from the floor. "But tomorrow you have a choice to make, Remmy, and I hope you make the right one. The smart one."

"Choice?" Remmy growled. "What kind of choice could I possibly have?"

"Fight or food," Jessica grinned. "It's up to you, because you're going to do one or be the other."

-27-

Looking for Cora's filthy Emo boyfriend was about the last thing in the world that Xander wanted to do. But he couldn't pass up a chance to get out of the camp, even if it meant pretending to look for Remmy. Why try to find the moron anyway? He had chosen to die and for what? To save Cora? She was a lost cause and Remmy surely could have outrun her. Xander would have. It was simple math. The faster one got to live, the slower one distracts the Reds.

It didn't matter. Remmy was probably dead or dying and Cora was having a mental breakdown. Xander was free to roam around, so all was right with the world as far as he was concerned. Left in the tent with nothing to do besides plan, Xander kept returning to one idea – the limo. The Emos had buried his mother and the ERC officer, but there was nothing done with the limo. Xander was sure that it was still in the field, slowly rusting in the same spot it had tumbled to a stop.

Somewhere behind him, Xander could hear the steps of an Emo guard, but they were distracted, weakened by emotion and concern. Xander shared none of these shortcomings, and focused on getting to the wrecked limo with the single mindedness afforded him through the small device implanted at the base of his neck.

Ducking into a thicket, Xander waited for the guard to pass. The thorns bit into his skin, but he remained still. Small rubies welled on the exposed skin of Xander's arms and legs before snaking downward in crooked zigzags. The guard continued down the path, eyes watchful for any sign of Remmy, but blind to Xander.

"So stupid," Xander grinned as he doubled back the way he had come. He would get to the limo, find what he needed and be back at the camp before anyone realized what was going on.

The sun sank lower in the sky, painting the woods in purpled shadows. It was strange, something Xander had never experienced. Sure, he had been in the woods before, but that was in the perfectly manicured parks scattered throughout the Stele. Those were little

LOVE BUG

more than paved paths flanked by decorative trees with colorful blossoms. Where Xander currently found himself had been left to grow unfettered by the meddling hand of man for centuries. Trees, as wide as three men, closed in on him. Anything could be hiding behind those trunks or in those darkening shadows. Xander had all of these thoughts, but none of the emotions to feel the fear. Rather, he simply accepted them as fact. His Em-Pak merrily chirped away as he picked his way closer to the scene of his mother's death.

"Finally," Xander said, having grown weary of the repetitive scenery of the woods. The twisted remains of the limo lay before him, a slight patina of rust on the upturned underside trying desperately to absorb the dying rays of the setting sun.

Broken glass crunched beneath Xander's shoes as he looked over the crash. It really was amazing that anyone had survived, let alone both Cora and himself, but Xander pushed these thoughts aside, allowing them to be cleansed by his Em-Pak. He was here for a purpose, a reason.

Climbing through the shattered window, Xander stopped to marvel at the amount of blood that had dried on the inside of the vehicle. It really must have been something to see, those disgusting Reds gunned down by a brave ERC officer. Xander still refused to believe Cora's ridiculous story about Remmy killing the Reds with a rock.

The limo had rolled over onto its roof, setting everything upside down. Xander cast a quick glance into the rear area where he had ridden, but saw nothing of value, just the litter of his mother and sister; surely, nothing worth taking with him. But the dashboard was a different story. There was most definitely something worth finding there.

Xander dropped to a squat on his knees, ignoring the pain that jabbed at him as he knelt on bits of broken safety glass. Grabbing the glove box, Xander yanked with all his might, but it refused to open. His Em-Pak beeped angrily.

"Come on," Xander grunted as he pressed his foot against the dash for leverage. With one final growl, he tore open the jammed glove box, but his foot shot sideways, colliding with the steering wheel. Xander felt his heart stop as a blaring blast of the car horn filled the field.

"Damn it," Xander cried and began feverishly sorting through the contents of the opened compartment. "Yes!" He grabbed the small radio, no bigger than a deck of cards. He remembered when his father had told him that all ERC vehicles were equipped with an emergency radio. It could be used to send an SOS signal or to radio the nearest ERC office, but he would need to get somewhere away from the camp, away from the forest and anything else that might muddy the signal. Xander's mind began to work overtime, trying to fit together the pieces of his plan. He was only going to have one chance to do this.

"Hey kid!" the guard yelled. "What the hell are you doing in there?" He pointed with the barrel of his rifle.

"Not as stupid as I thought," Xander smirked and slipped the radio into his sock before pulling his pant leg back into place. He crawled out of the wrecked limo. "Remmy knew where this was. I thought he might have gone here to hide. Seemed like a good place. Don't you think?"

"Yeah, I guess so," the guard agreed, "but you shouldn't be running off like that. There could still be Reds around here."

"Oh," Xander exclaimed, feigning the concern of which he was incapable. "We should probably get back to the camp then, shouldn't we?"

"Let's go," the guard snapped. "And keep your eyes peeled on the way back for any sign of Remmy or the Reds, okay?"

"Of course," Xander smiled, his voice syrupy and sweet. These Emos were exactly as stupid as he thought.

-28-

The Emo camp buzzed with a mix of suppressed anger and sadness. No loss was easy, but Remmy being taken hit everyone hard. Cora tried to comfort Remmy's mother, but with no practice, she found herself doing little more than uttering a few sentences and crying alongside the woman. Maybe that's what it was supposed to be like Cora wondered? Maybe in moments like these there was no point in trying to string words together? They would probably fail to capture the magnitude of the loss or situation, so why bother? Cora sat with Remmy's mother until she became exhausted from her crying and slipped into a fitful sleep.

Cora quietly slipped out of the tent and found Remmy's father standing outside with a few other men. When he saw Cora, he stopped talking and walked over to her.

"Thank you," Remmy's father nodded. "She always wanted a daughter, but having kids was so risky. I'm sure that meant a lot to her. I'm really bad at that kind of stuff."

"Doesn't mean it wouldn't help," Cora responded, but immediately wished she had kept her mouth shut. Emotions were making her words faster than her thoughts and she had no way to control them. "Sorry, I didn't mean to –"

"No, no," Remmy's father cut in. "You're right. It's cowardice, not a lack of skill that keeps me from trying to comfort her." His eyes glistened from the nearby fire and tears began to roll. "I guess it just feels like if we don't talk about it that it's not really real then. You know? Like if, we don't say anything that Remmy might just come walking right into the middle of camp. I don't know. It's stupid, I guess."

"Not really," Cora replied. "I can understand not wanting to talk about it, but she needs you."

"I know," Remmy's father nodded. "You're right."

"I'm going to see Samuel," Cora added. "You want me to come by after and check on her?"

"Thanks, but I'll take it from here," Remmy's father said sheepishly and then added, "What I said before, Cora, I meant it. I really think Remmy loved you."

"Thanks," Cora nodded, "I hope he did."

Cora turned and began walking through the camp. Every group she passed would fall silent as she passed. Were they blaming her for Remmy? Cora wanted to scream at each and every one of them that she felt responsible enough and didn't need their judgment. She hoped that Samuel would have some advice, some small piece of wisdom that would make what she was feeling slightly less terrible.

The hospital tent was empty, all patients having been patched up and loaded into vehicles just in case the Reds returned. Samuel sat at a table in the rear of the tent, a small gas lantern throwing a golden glow around his stooped figure like a halo.

"Samuel?" Cora asked as she stepped into the tent. She still found it strange to think of him as her grandfather and had yet to use the word. Her entire life had been shaped by Samuel's fake death and sitting down with him still felt a little like conversing with a ghost.

"Back here, Cora," Samuel waved, not looking up from his work.

"What are you doing?" Cora asked, not really interested in his work, but looking for any kind of distraction.

"We'll get to that soon enough," Samuel smiled, "but why don't we start with how you're doing."

"Terrible," Cora muttered as she kicked at some invisible object on the floor with the toe her boot. "Remmy's dead and it's my fault. How else should I feel?"

"It's not your fault," Samuel said, "You can't put that on yourself, Cora. If you do, it'll destroy you. I promise you that I know where that road leads."

"What do you mean?" Cora demanded.

"Look around you, Cora," Samuel motioned with his arms. She got the feeling he was speaking about things far larger than the tent and even the camp. "All of this is my fault. My creation made all of this. How many people died because of what I made? How much blood is on my hands?"

"But you were only trying to help," Cora argued. "How could you have known the ERC could totally screw up your invention?"

"And how could you have known that Reds were near the waterfall?" Samuel asked. He had a way of getting Cora to see his point, of guiding her there without forcing it or making it seem condescending. "Neither you nor Remmy knew the Reds would be there. You can't blame yourself for things beyond your control. Life is full of unknown variables and we have to do our best to deal with them."

"Yeah," Cora muttered, her voice devoid of conviction. "But he never would have tried to slow the Reds down if I wasn't there. If I hadn't been there, Remmy would have just outrun them and warned the camp. Remmy would still be alive if it wasn't for me."

"I know that's how you feel right now," Samuel extended a hand and placed it on Cora's shoulder, "but that doesn't make it real. And besides, who said Remmy was dead?"

Cora tilted her head. Samuel had always seemed a bit odd. How could he not be a little strange considering the insanity that shaped his life? But claiming that Remmy was still alive was not only insane - it was cruel.

"Why would you say that?" Cora growled with more intensity than she intended.

"Because, I think he might still be alive," Samuel stated matter-of-factly. "That's what I've been working on." He motioned towards his computer. A large digital map covered the screen. Colored dots, red, blue and yellow were clustered across the map.

"What is that?" Cora asked.

"I've been tracking the movement of the Reds with these red dots, the ERC with the blue ones and other camps like ours with the yellow," Samuel explained. It felt weird to think of the camp as 'ours', but Cora suddenly realized that she had come to think of it as hers, as her home. "I figured that there had to be some sort of pattern to the Reds and that they couldn't be so random. It's also a good way to keep tabs on the movement of ERC troops."

"How?" Cora asked. It was amazing to see how many yellow dots were on the screen. She would have never imagined that so many Emos were nearby.

"I hacked into an ERC satellite," Samuel grinned. "I had helped program the thing, so it wasn't really that difficult."

"But how can you tell the difference between the groups?" Cora gasped. "They're all just people aren't they?"

"Well, yes," Samuel nodded. "But there's a slight temperature variation between the three. You see the virus raises the Reds' core temperature to over one hundred degrees, also adding to their red appearance. Em-Paks have the opposite effect, decreasing the core temperature. You never knew the difference, but those early citizens who were harnessed later in life used to complain constantly about feeling cold. Then there's us. We're within the normal range for human beings. Once I routed a patch program into the satellite, it was easy to zero in on certain temperature signatures."

"Aren't you worried that the ERC would find out how to do the same thing?" Cora demanded. "You could have just made their job that much easier."

"True," Samuel responded, "except for the fact that I triple encrypted the program and attached a failsafe. It's completely hidden in the coding for other programs, but if they ever find it and try to hack the file, it will self-destruct and disable the entire satellite. It's safe, Cora. I'm not making the mistake of underestimating or trusting the ERC ever again."

"The map is impressive," Cora admitted, "but what does that have to do with Remmy?"

"This," Samuel smiled and zoomed in on a large section of red dots. A small, faint yellow dot could be seen amidst them. It was very close to a single red dot. "I think that yellow dot might be Remmy."

"How could that be?" Cora's voice cracked. "The Reds don't take prisoners."

"No," Samuel agreed. "They usually don't, but that too has been something that I have been thinking a great deal about lately. You see, after you arrived, I knew that the Reds had changed, evolved, if you will. They had never worked in unison before, but it was naïve to believe that the virus would never mutate. That's what viruses do, right?"

"Sure," Cora shrugged. She had no idea what Samuel was talking about.

"Viruses change constantly," Samuel continued, "so it stands to reason that the Reds might change as well. I believe that they have become more than screaming, mindless monsters and that they are developing, possibly even creating their own society."

"Seriously?" Cora questioned. "The ERC always taught us that the Reds were like rabid animals."

"And what did they teach you about Emos?" Samuel smirked.

Cora felt her face flush, those prickly waves of heat dancing on the back of her neck and cheeks. "Yeah, I guess that's a good point."

"So I began to consider how the Reds might develop their rules, their way of life," Samuel said. "And the only logical foundation I can think of which the Reds would base their culture upon is fighting. They surely are becoming or have become a warrior society."

"What about Remmy?" Cora demanded, growing tired of the long-winded explanation.

"You said that he grabbed a rock," Samuel answered, "that he turned to fight. My guess is that he fought and somehow this meant something to the Reds. Maybe they respected Remmy for it. They must have captured him and taken him back to their camp. I have been monitoring this group for a while now because their movements seemed more organized. There had never been anything other than red dots. That is, until the day after you and Remmy were attacked. I'm not a gambling man, Cora, but I'd be willing to bet that Remmy is there."

"So Remmy is still alive?" Cora almost shouted.

"So it would seem," Samuel smiled. "Now all we have to figure out is how we're going to get him back."

"Thank you, Grandpa!" Cora cried as she wrapped her arms around Samuel. The word felt natural, like it had always been waiting to be spoken. Samuel, her grandfather, had given her hope. It was small, but it was hope. Remmy was alive, surrounded by Reds, but alive. Cora had never felt hope before, had never known that airy, lightheaded feeling that made anything seem possible, but it came naturally to her. She would rescue Remmy and bring him back. He had saved her and she owed him. She would see him again and kiss him again. She loved Remmy. She knew it before, but her heart screamed it now. With these feelings, Cora could accomplish anything, even the impossible task that was saving Remmy from an entire army of Reds.

-29-

"Time to eat, Remmy," Jessica grinned, her shark-like teeth glittering like polished ivory in the moonlight. She held a crude wooden bowl with some sort of brown stew lazily steaming away in the middle of it.

"I don't want that," Remmy snapped, "get that crap away from me."

"Suit yourself," Jessica shrugged. She stepped into the shack and shut the door behind her. In the darkness, Remmy was tempted to pretend that she was still his friend and still the girl he used to know, but the moment she talked, cutting apart her words on rows of dagger-like teeth, the illusion was shattered. "You're only getting food because you're going to fight tomorrow. Trust me, in the arena, you're going to need your strength."

"I'm not fighting for your amusement tomorrow," Remmy spat from where he slumped against the wall.

"Amusement?" Jessica chuckled. "Well, yes, I guess it is what passes for entertainment around here, but that's not the real reason you'll be in there."

"So, then why am I?" Remmy demanded.

"To prove yourself," Jessica explained. "You showed some real promise when you dropped Tam with that rock. He's second in command around here, probably will be the chief one day, if Hatch ever let's him. Besting one of our toughest fighters is what saved your life."

"Lot of good that did me," Remmy said darkly.

"If you hadn't done that, you'd be dead and would have been taken for food," Jessica answered. "You have a chance to prove yourself tomorrow, to fight hard enough to change. You've got a chance to become one of us. When you get in there tomorrow, Remmy, you need to fight, to get angry. Allow the change to happen."

"You mean become infected," Remmy snapped.

"Look at it however you need to," Jessica stated simply. "Remmy, you have a shot, a chance to live. It's more than we give most people. If you refuse to fight, there's only one outcome."

"What the hell do you care?" Remmy grunted. "You'd just as soon eat me."

"Circle of life," Jessica shrugged. "Do I want to eat you? No, I'd rather you joined us. But will I eat you? I will if you leave us no other choice. We've all got a right to live and to survive. But, Remmy, I'm still me. I'm still Jessica. The change doesn't erase everything. I still remember what it was like to be your friend. That's why I'm trying to help save you, Remmy."

Remmy paused before he answered. Was it possible that Jessica really was trying to save him? Did she really want to keep him safe and this was the only way she knew how?

"Or we could speed all this up and I could kill you right now," Jessica lunged forward, spilling the stew and gnashed her teeth together mere inches from Remmy's neck. He heard the loud *clack* of Jessica's pointed teeth and felt the air move across the exposed skin of his neck. Jessica rocked back onto the floor, a wicked toothy grin stretched across her face. "Relax, Remmy, I was only kidding! You earned your chance in the arena. You'll get a fair shot, just like I did."

"You went into this arena?" Remmy asked, some small memory of Jessica triggering a spark of concern. "What did you have to do?"

"I was put in the arena a few years ago and what I had to do was win. It's what you'll have to do tomorrow, if you want to survive," Jessica said, as if she were simply reporting the day's weather. "It's how we keep our numbers up."

"Um, okay," Remmy grumbled. "Can't you just *make* more Reds instead of throwing innocent people into your arena?"

Jessica laughed as she played with the empty bowl and spoon. "It's not really that simple. For a while, we thought that it would be possible, but there were too many unknowns. There was no way to know if the baby would be born one of us or if we'd have to wait and turn them. But then none of those questions mattered because we finally pieced together that the virus leaves us incapable of having children."

"So you're all infertile," Remmy clarified. "You have to make new Reds from people you kidnap."

"Pretty much," Jessica shrugged, "but only those like you, the ones that show promise. The others are used to stock the pantry." Jessica snorted and then added. "We don't really have a pantry."

"Hence the whole 'fight or food' lecture," Remmy spat. "I get the whole making new Reds thing, but why bother eating the others?"

"Good question," Jessica smiled and ran her tongue across her wicked looking teeth. "And one that I really don't have an answer for. It's just something that we're compelled to do, something that the virus makes us do. I guess it's nature. Birds gotta sing, bees gotta buzz, and Reds gotta eat."

"Lovely," Remmy spat sarcastically.

"Like I said, Remmy, look at it however you need to," Jessica shrugged. "I really do hope you make the right decision tomorrow. That you decide to fight instead of to be food." Jessica got up and walked towards the door. She paused in the doorway, framed in silvery moonlight. "Sleep tight, Remmy. Don't let the bedbugs bite." She clacked her teeth together and slammed the door. Even with the door closed, Remmy could hear her laughing and gnashing her teeth.

-30-

Eldritch found himself oddly bored. His Em-Pak controlled and dissipated emotions and feelings and boredom was not one of them. In fact, Eldritch suspected that his Em-Pak and a lack of emotions made his boredom even worse, removing the very things that might offer some small distraction. Numerous administrative tasks always need to be accomplished and minute details needed his careful attention, but the excitement of overthrowing the ERC Council had waned and left him empty. The distractions of his position provided some degree of relief, but not much. He needed something new to turn his attention towards, and focus on, or otherwise he would become no better than the group of people he had just deposed.

For lack of a better option, Eldritch punched a few keys on his computer and brought up the video feed from his family's car crash. Maybe some small splinter of affection laid buried deep within, hidden from his Em-Pak or maybe he was just bored. Either way, Eldritch found himself staring at a topsy-turvy world through the dashboard camera of limo. There was really nothing new to see. The ERC officer covered in blood, crawling out and getting killed by Reds. That nasty little Emo boy showing up to do God knows what. If only there was something in the video that Eldritch could use, some small bit of information that would give him new direction. And perhaps even more importantly, give Captain Ortiz and his men direction.

Eldritch had trusted Ortiz, but now wondered about the man's loyalties. Ortiz had already overthrown one set of rulers, so would it really be a stretch for him to do it again, especially now that he knew how? If Eldritch was in Ortiz's position, he knew that the thought would be forming in his mind. It was the logical next step. Ortiz surely would desire the control and power that he had just helped Eldritch achieve.

Eldritch broke from his thoughts and cued a series of Em-Pak Identification numbers. Running a quick program put the numbers in a sort of electronic lockbox, one that was linked directly to Eldritch's own Em-Pak. Should his ever cease to function and sense his vital signals, the lockbox would open and deactivate the loaded identification numbers. It wasn't a perfect plan, but it would ensure that if Ortiz or his men ever got smart enough or brazen enough to kill him that Eldritch could at least take them with him.

The other small splinter of worry that festered and rotted within Eldritch's mind was what to do with the Em-Paks. His father's notes had clearly said that they would eventually lose their effectiveness, but was that because of a body building resistance or because of the Em-Pak's signal weakening? A physical resistance to the Em-Pak would be far more difficult to manage, but increasing the signal should be easy enough. All Eldritch needed was a guinea pig.

Pressing the intercom, Eldritch waited impatiently for the three or four seconds it took his aide to respond.

"Yes, sir, Mr. Eldritch?" the aide's voice sounded robotic and tinny through the intercom speaker. "How can I help you, sir?"

"I need you in my office," Eldritch barked. "Now." He could hear his aide's chair push back from the desk outside his office doors even before the echo of his words dissipated.

"Yes, sir?" the aide asked as he stepped through the large oak double doors. "What can I do for you, sir?"

"Just stand there, please," Eldritch said. His aide's Em-Pak began beeping away, correcting his nerves, no doubt. Eldritch figured it probably was more his use of the word please than it was his odd request that caused his aide's Em-Pak to work overtime.

"Okay," his aide said slowly. "Yes, sir. I can do that."

"Good," Eldritch said without looking up. He began punching keys on his computer. "Do you feel anything? Anything different?"

"No sir," his aide responded. "Should I?"

"We shall see," Eldritch mumbled and hit more keys. "Maybe if I turn up the frequency on…" Eldritch muttered to himself and hit a sequence of buttons.

His aide suddenly released a scream and fell to the floor. Eldritch momentarily worried that he had allowed the man to become infected and that he would have a Red to worry about soon. But as he stood up from his desk, gun in hand, Eldritch could see the man rolling back and forth on the polished stone floor. He was in pain, but not infected.

"Hmm," Eldritch pondered. "Well that's good, not helpful, but still worth knowing." He punched a few more keys, dialing back the intensity of the signal to his aide's Em-Pak. The man immediately stopped screaming and stood up from the floor. His eyes were wide, unblinking and glassy.

"What do you feel now?" Eldritch asked.

"Nothing, sir," the aide said flatly. "I feel nothing...what are your orders, sir?" The man had the effect of a robot, his breathing barely detectable and face completely blank. "Excellent," Eldritch nodded and began working on a large-scale version of his new Em-Pak program.

-31-

"We're going to get him back," Cora said firmly, the eyes of those gathered around her going wide with disbelief. "Remmy is alive."

The other Emos murmured amongst themselves, but no voices spoke up in support or protest of Cora's plan. Samuel stood beside her, his presence quiet and strong. With Xander kept in his tent, it was safe for Samuel to be outside of the hospital tent.

"We need to move," Samuel spoke up. "There is a large group of Reds heading this way. It's not the group that has Remmy, but I think they may be moving to meet up with that group. If there's any chance of saving Remmy, it's before the two groups join up."

"What do you mean *another* group of Reds?" someone in the crowd shouted.

Samuel examined the crowd, trying to determine how much to tell them. He had sworn Cora to secrecy regarding his access to the ERC satellite. It was not that Samuel distrusted anyone in the camp. They stood to gain nothing by altering the ERC to his recent activities. What worried Samuel was how the others would react knowing that multiple groups of Reds were converging in one spot. Soon after he had accessed the satellite, Samuel noticed movement amongst the Reds. All seemed to be migrating towards the group that held Remmy. This information would surely cause panic, so Samuel lied. There were far more than two groups of Reds. From what he had seen, there were at least six more heading directly through the Emo camp on their way to converge with the other Reds. Samuel had to tell them just enough to get them to move, but not enough to cause wide spread panic.

"The rest of you need to pack up and move," Samuel continued. "I have explained to Remmy's father where the best place is to move our camp." Cora and Samuel had known that Remmy's father would want to go, but they needed him to lead the others. He could be trusted to keep the others focused. His example was one they would follow. If too many central figures from the camp left to go after Remmy, Samuel worried that, the group would fall apart, making themselves easy targets for the large groups of Reds converging on the area.

Remmy's father had taken a great deal of convincing to stay behind, but Cora and Samuel had persisted. What was the point of saving Remmy if there was nothing to bring him back to? It was equally important to ensure the survival of the group, and once Samuel had relented and shown Remmy's father the large numbers of Reds scattered across the computer screen, he reluctantly agreed to stay behind and lead the others.

"So who's going? Who's going to get Remmy?" a boy about his age demanded. Cora couldn't tell from the tone in his voice if he was angry or volunteering. Maybe it was both.

"I'm going," Cora snapped, glaring at the boy. "So is Samuel."

"And what about your brother?" someone shouted. "We're just supposed to take him along with us? He's putting us all at risk." Cora and Samuel had expected this, but hoped that no one would broach the question. They had no argument against this point. Xander was a risk and with Cora gone, no one could be held responsible for him.

"I'll watch him," Remmy's father growled. "The boy won't be any trouble."

"The boy is nothing but trouble!" someone else shouted. "I say we leave him here for the Reds. Otherwise, you take him with you."

"Fine!" Cora screamed. "Just shut up! We were taking him anyway." She knew that Xander couldn't be trusted. She also knew that Remmy's father would do his best to protect her brother and limit the amount of trouble he caused, but Xander was devious. She needed to keep him where she could watch him, but this meant revealing Samuel to him.

Samuel had said that it was time. Time for Xander to know the truth, but Cora still worried. But honestly, there really wasn't much Xander could do with the knowledge, other than get angry and even that his Em-Pak would handle...probably.

"The three of you? An elderly doctor, a teenage girl, and an emotionless city boy?" someone teased from the crowd. "That hardly seems like a rescue party."

"I'm a little more than just some elderly doctor," Samuel smiled. "And Cora will do just fine. A smaller group has a better chance of slipping in undetected. This is a rescue mission, not a war. We get Remmy and we get out. If we don't come back, Remmy's father will tell you what to do."

Rumbles passed through the crowd. People were understandably worried, but the discussion was over. Cora and the remains of her family were going to save Remmy.

-32-

The ground shook with the fevered stomps of countless Reds. Remmy tried to remain calm, but the promise of violence reverberated through the air, jangling his nerves with a strange energy. Jessica pushed him towards the arena.

The arena was little more than a massive circle of old rusted school buses, placed end to end. Large patches of brown rust stretched down the sides of the buses like old wounds, the blood long since dried and turned brown. A slightly less rusted tow truck had been pushed to the side, creating a small opening that yawned like the hungry mouth of some terrible beast eagerly waiting to consume Remmy. Row upon row of Reds clung to the sides and roofs of the buses. Heads darted in and out of the broken windows, all trying to get a glimpse of the day's entertainment or perhaps the evening's meal. Wild faces, smeared with red paint glared at Remmy as he came closer, each wilder and more vicious looking than the next.

Remmy's feet involuntarily stopped, his heels digging into the dirt as if some invisible force was trying to prevent him from entering the circle of rusted buses, but Jessica shoved him forward. The Reds began howling with laughter. Jeers and insults were launched from the perimeter of the arena, calling Remmy scared, weak, or worst of all, dinner. Remmy tried to block out the noise, but it overwhelmed him, rattling his insides and shaking loose feelings of doubt and hopelessness.

"Fight or food, Remmy," Jessica hissed in his ear. "Make the right choice."

There was no way for Remmy to know what waited for him inside the arena, but one thing was clear – the next few minutes would determine whether he lived or died. Something ancient, some ingrained shred of evolution screamed in Remmy's head, demanding that he prepare himself to fight, to kill. It demanded that he recognize the gravity of his current situation and do whatever was needed to survive.

Another piece of Remmy's mind pleaded with him to hold on to who he was, and remember what he had been taught. He found himself able to think of nothing other than Cora and that brief kiss they shared beside the waterfall. That moment sank into his soul, joining with his heart and defining who he was, or at least who he had hoped he could be. Cora was his hope, his sign that the world was still good and that there was still a reason to strive for a future greater than what he had been given. Bitter tears stung the corners of Remmy's eyes as he felt his future, and Cora slipping through his fingers, a little more with each step closer to the arena.

"Stop it! Get your head in it!" Jessica growled and slapped Remmy across the face. "There's no time for daydreaming! Stop showing weakness. Get angry, get angry right now, Remmy! Whatever it is that you're thinking about, forget it. Let it go right now! Anger is the only thing that's going to save you in there." She snapped her dagger-like teeth to drive her point home. A wicked smile spread across Jessica's face. Remmy found it hard to guess Jessica's intentions and even harder to pretend that he cared about them. She had been his friend once, but that person was gone, buried along with the Red that killed her family. Jessica was a Red, a monster, and currently walking him towards what would undoubtedly be the most excruciating experience of his short life.

Remmy nodded, but was unable to forget about Cora. If he had to fight to live, then so be it. Remmy was willing to do anything to see Cora again. The things that waited for Remmy inside the arena would undoubtedly change him, possibly twist him into someone that Cora wouldn't recognize, but Remmy knew that no other choice remained. He only hoped that if he were lucky enough to see Cora again that she wouldn't be repulsed by what she saw.

These thoughts and countless others were drowned out as Remmy was pushed into the arena. The tow truck was rolled back into place, closing off the only way in or out. An entire chorus of screams rose to a fevered crescendo, suddenly falling silent. Remmy's eyes went wide as he finally saw what awaited him inside the arena.

-33-

"It is the duty of every citizen to ensure that they have a functioning Em-Pak. It is the privilege and honor of every citizen to report those who do not. To remove one's Em-Pak is to choose death. The Emotions Regulatory Commission will not tolerate such traitorous behavior. All citizens must adhere to the Citizens' Safety Protocol. The virus cannot be allowed within the walls of your city. The Reds cannot be allowed to return. Emotions are weakness, flaws that lead to only one end. It is the duty of every citizen to ensure that they have a functioning Em-Pak."

Eldritch silently mouthed the words of the recording. He had helped the ERC Council write it, let alone had heard it enough times to know it by heart. He was sure there were probably nights that he quietly mumbled it in his sleep. But he hated it, detested what it represented. It was a constant reminder of how his plans had stagnated. What was the point of deposing the ERC Council and taking over leadership of the ERC if he was simply going to do the exact things the Council had done?

"Status quo," Eldritch muttered as he sorted through a stack of papers. "Everything and everyone, nothing more than status quo." He knew nothing of interest or importance awaited him buried within the pile of papers, rather sorting through it was a habit born out of boredom. Eldritch sighed and dropped the papers onto his desk.

Everything was running smoothly. Order had returned. Ortiz and his men periodically reminded people to stay in line and to fear the combined threat of the Reds and Emos, but still something was missing.

"Coffee, sir," Eldritch's aide said flatly, as he walked into the office. He held a small gold tray. A delicate china cup and a small saucer with three cubes of sugar rattled faintly as he walked across the room. The man had become little more than a robot since Eldritch had played with the signal to his Em-Pak. Not much for conversation, but dutiful to a fault. Eldritch found that his aide was forgetting to eat and bathe, focusing instead on his administrative tasks. His aide's dedication was admirable, but his smell was not.

Eldritch commanded him to return to his housing unit, eat something and wash up. The aide arrived back in the office in under an hour, clearly having followed through with Eldritch's orders, but what amazed Eldritch was the speed at which his aide had accomplished these errands. Lacking status and money meant living in one of the city's outer housing units. Transport to his aide's block would have taken at least fifteen minutes.

"How did you accomplish that so quickly?" Eldritch questioned as his aide set down his coffee. "There's no way a transport would have gotten you there and back in under an hour, let alone allowed time to shower and eat."

"The transport would have taken too long, sir," his aide responded.

"So how then did you get home?" Eldritch asked.

"Ran, sir," his aide said flatly. "Running allows for a more direct route. I ate in the shower and then ran back. I estimated that this plan would require the least amount of time away from the office and my duties, sir."

"You ran?" Eldritch snapped. "How is that possible? It's miles from here. You'd be exhausted."

"Exhaustion is simply a state of mind, Mr. Eldritch," his aide responded matter-of-factly. The sweat dotting his forehead spoke otherwise. "With the recent changes to my Em-Pak, I am no longer a slave to my mind and body. Now, it serves me, sir."

"And you serve me," Eldritch smiled, a cold predatory look settling across his gaze. Slowly, the pieces began to fall into place and boredom no longer seemed to be an issue. "So you are able to run fast. That's good, but can you do anything else? Any other super human feats?"

"What would you like to see, sir?" his aide asked.

"I don't know," Eldritch thought for a moment. "Jump high."

Eldritch's aide paused for a moment, all of his muscles tensing, coiling to release in one motion. The man sprang ten feet into the air, well over what he should have been able to accomplish, before landing on the floor. "Was that acceptable, sir?" his aide asked, limping slightly.

"Are you injured?" Eldritch asked, more from a stance of scientific interest as opposed to concern.

"Not sure, Mr. Eldritch," his aide answered as he flexed his foot. "I may have torn the tendon or perhaps a muscle, but I can try again if you would like."

"That's absurd," Edlritch scoffed. "You managed to jump high enough to tear your tendon and you're still willing to try again?" Now Eldritch's interest was really peaked. His aide was clearly injured, and by all accounts should be on the ground writhing in pain. Yet, all the man was doing was waiting for another order, even if it meant greater pain.

"Of course, I will try again, sir," his aide answered simply.

"That's insane. Completely insane," Eldritch smiled, his Em-Pak trying in vain to tamper down his sudden bursts of self-satisfaction. "You're telling me that no matter how ridiculous the command is, and that no matter what the consequences are, you'll follow it?"

"No request should be viewed as such, sir," the aide replied. "What command could be seen as so ridiculous that it shouldn't be followed, Mr. Eldritch?"

"Oh, I don't know," Eldritch thought. "Ram your head through the wall? Something like that." Before Eldritch could stop his aide, the man broke into a sprint across the large room, gaining more and more speed with each step. A sickening *snap–crunch* echoed through the room.

Eldritch walked across his office, his eyes wide with amazement. Had his aide really just killed himself trying to run his head through a concrete wall? Was the new program really that effective? The toe of his shoe nudged the crumpled pile that had once been his aide. The man remained still. Eldritch's Em-Pak could barely keep the smile from stretching across his face.

Grabbing his phone from his pocket, Eldritch quickly punched the keys to call Captain Ortiz. "Ortiz?" Eldritch snapped. "I need you and fifty of your most trusted, most dedicated soldiers at my office in twenty."

"Understood, sir," Ortiz's voice chimed through the phone. "Is this another Emo excursion to be undertaken, Mr. Eldritch, sir? Anything I need to prepare the men for, sir? Will there be anything else?"

"No on both accounts, Captain," Eldritch lied. "Just bring the men. That is all." But there would be something else, something that would truly grant Eldritch the power he sought. There would be so much more to follow if his next round of experiments proved fruitful.

Eldritch returned to his computer and switched off the citywide feed of the ERC recording. There would no longer be a need to remind the citizens who they served.

-34-

"Xander, get out here!" Cora's voice barked from outside the tent. She really was so bossy. Was this what big sisters were like without an Em-Pak to correct their irrational behavior, Xander mused, as he toyed with the small radio transmitter. The battery life was limited, but it was still worth the juice to flick the switch and see the lights blink to life. Each small flashing green LED light was a beacon, a lighthouse, guiding Xander back to safe port, back to the Stele, back to his father. The few remaining red lights on the radio signaled that he needed to find an area free of those troublesome trees where the broadcast would be stronger. Xander tucked the radio back into his sock and straightened the wrinkles in his pant leg just as Cora burst into the tent.

"Didn't you hear me calling you?" she snapped.

"Hear you?" Xander asked flatly. "Yes, I heard you. I'm sure everyone heard that shrill banshee shriek of a voice. I just didn't care."

Cora flushed red and she had to take a few deep breaths before continuing. Xander was awful. There really was no away around. Remmy had told her that other kids complained about their siblings, especially younger ones, but she suspected that Xander was easily the worst in the history of siblings.

"Get outside, you brat," Cora pulled aside the flaps with one hand and angrily pointed with the other. "We're leaving."

"Leaving?" Xander asked. Cora couldn't help but notice the ping of her brother's Em-Pak.

"Don't get your hopes up," Cora added, "it's not what you think."

"I don't care where it is," Xander answered. "Leaving is good enough."

"We're going to get Remmy," Cora continued.

"Oh," Xander mumbled as he slunk out of the tent. "Wonderful." His eyes bore into the man standing next to his sister.

Cora almost immediately heard Xander's Em-Pak going into overdrive. She smiled, a sense of satisfaction at having thrown off

Xander's attempts to be so nonplussed and cold. Maybe there was still hope for her brother?

"What kind of nasty Emo trick is this?" Xander demanded. His Em-Pak chirped furiously as his fingers balled into fists and then relaxed after each mechanical chime. "Who are you? This is impossible! It's a trick! A disgusting Emo trick!" Xander turned to storm back into the tent, but Cora blocked his escape.

"You need to hear what he has to say, Xander," Cora said. "Please just listen to him. He really is our grandfather and that really is Samuel Eldritch."

Tears momentarily formed in the corners of Xander's eyes and then vanished just as suddenly with one beep of his Em-Pak.

"Fine," Xander growled and turned to face the man who looked like his grandfather, claimed to be his grandfather, but surely was an imposter.

"Xander," Samuel said slowly, "Cora is telling you the truth. We hid it from you because we didn't know how you'd react, but time has forced our hand. Cora and I are going to try to save Remmy and for your own safety, you're coming too."

"My own safety?" Xander scoffed. "I'm safer here where only the Emos want to kill me. Why would I risk my life for that worthless Emo, whatever his name?"

Cora's hand moved under its own volition, as if directed by some unseen force. Xander's head snapped violently to the side as Cora's hand made contact with his cheek. A bright red outline glowed, as if highlighting the attack.

Xander looked momentarily shocked, but a flat expression soon returned to his face. "As I was saying," Xander continued, "why would I risk myself for him?"

"Because he did it for you!" Cora snapped. "Or have you forgotten that Remmy was the one that pulled you from the wrecked limo? He could have just as easily left you there to be killed by the Reds."

"He should have," Xander shrugged. "It's what I would have done if the roles were reversed."

"Enough, Xander," Samuel said, his voice strong, but not angry. Samuel knew that even with his Em-Pak in place, Xander was dealing with an overwhelming situation and couldn't help but feel sad for his grandson. "You're right that it's not safe for you out there, but it's not safe for you here either. You're coming with us. It's not open for discussion."

"You think just because you look like my grandfather that you can tell me what to do, old man?" Xander sneered. "Please, next I'll be taking orders from Cora."

"See," Cora grumbled, "I told you it wasn't worth it. We should just leave him here and whatever happens is his own stupid fault!"

Xander opened his mouth to continue to protest, but the pressing of the radio transmitter against his leg silenced his words. Going with them was exactly what he needed to do. Let them lead him away from the camp to somewhere he could trigger the radio signal and contact the ERC.

"Fine," Xander seethed, playing up his disapproval. "But how do I really know that you're Samuel Eldritch? How can I trust you?" Xander really cared little for the answer. If this man was his grandfather, at least genetically, he was nothing like the man he had idolized, more importantly, nothing like his father.

Samuel told Xander the abbreviated version of his story, quickly bringing the boy up to speed with Cora and leaving out the bit about hacking into ERC satellites. "You've got to understand, Xander that the Em-Paks were never meant to be a permanent fix," Samuel concluded. "But you've got a choice. You didn't have the choice to have the Em-Pak implanted, but you do have a choice whether or not you keep it. Cora and I cannot and will not make that decision for you."

"Oh, here we go," Xander rolled his eyes. "I was waiting for this to come full circle. Waiting for you to try and play my heart strings."

"What heart?" Cora laughed. "No one is trying to make you do anything, you little monster." She wanted to love Xander, and feel close to him, but he made it nearly impossible.

"Cora, that's enough," Samuel said.

"Don't," Cora warned him. "You're our grandfather and I like you, I do, but don't try to parent me."

"Fair enough," Samuel conceded, "I've been little more than a shadow in your lives and you're right, I shouldn't try to parent you, but we're wasting time. We need to get moving." Samuel flipped up the screen of a small computer strapped to his wrist. It was hardly bigger than a large wristwatch, but he had programmed all of his data into it. "They're on the move, Cora. We need to go if we're going to stay ahead of them."

"On the move? Who?" Xander demanded.

"The Reds," Cora answered.

"All the groups are moving towards each other," Samuel added. "They seem to be meeting up for some reason, so we need to go now if there's any hope of saving Remmy."

Xander could have cared less about saving Remmy; he was just another outlaw, another misguided, filthy Emo terrorist. But getting away from the camp and to a place where he could activate the radio was something that Xander cared about with every fiber of his being. He was willing to do anything if it held even the slightest promise of his rescue and return to the city, his father, and the way life should be.

"This just keeps getting better and better," Xander spat acerbically. "I can't believe that I'm going to help you save a filthy Emo, but what choice do I really have? Let's just get going before you tell me anything else."

Xander's Em-Pak beeped. Cora and Samuel wrote it off as nervousness, nothing more than fear. It was easy enough to believe that Xander would be worried about what lay before them, because Cora was. Had they known that his Em-Pak was battling feelings of joy and excitement, they may have reconsidered their decision to take Xander with them.

-35-

The shouts of the Reds on the tops of the buses fell silent. A large metal box sat at the far end of the arena. Remmy had no idea what was inside, held back by the rusted sheet metal door, but it couldn't be good.

"Hey, food!" one of the Reds shouted, "Better grab a weapon quick!" All the other Reds began laughing hysterically, even Jessica.

The large Red that Remmy had injured, Tam, stood atop the box, a shark-like smile craved into his face. His nose hooked to the left at a painful angle. Remmy took some small bit of solace knowing that he had done that.

Tam raised his hand and the crowd once again fell silent. "We'll start out easy. See if this boy really has the salt to become one of us." He reached down and pulled up the sheet of metal closing the front of the box.

Three small children scuttled out of the box. The children couldn't have been older than five or six years old. They were covered with mud and squinted as if even the pale moonlight hurt their eyes. Remmy figured that the Reds must have captured the children for this purpose, to make someone do something so horrible to survive that they couldn't help but become angry, and allow the infection in. Remmy felt a burst of disgust and anger in his gut. He wasn't going to do it. He would refuse, even if it meant death. He fought to control the anger, and remember that the Reds wanted him to lose control.

"I'm not going to kill children!" Remmy screamed, looking at the Reds on the edges of the arena. "Just kill me, because I won't do it."

"We won't have to kill you," Tam grinned, his yellowed teeth catching the light and glistening wickedly.

The three children crouched on all fours, rubbing their eyes, but appeared to be acclimating to the arena and the light. The children hopped forward, a strange look etched into their young faces.

Remmy scanned the perimeter of the arena and saw Jessica behind him. She was sitting next to a lithe woman covered in red paint. The woman had the predatory smile of a jungle cat and the look of a conquering hero. Remmy figured that she must be Hatch, the leader of the Reds. A thin, curved sword hung from Hatch's belt, dark stains speckled the leather braided around the handle, stains that could only be one thing.

Jessica motioned towards the length of wood that lay at Remmy's feet, urging him to pick it up. Remmy shook his head. There was no way he was going to bludgeon three children to survive. Death was a better choice.

"No," Remmy said firmly, staring at what had once been his friend. Hatch laughed and pointed, whispering something into Jessica's ear that made her laugh as well.

Remmy thought they were pointing at him, mocking his refusal to commit such atrocious acts, but as he glared at the two, he realized that they were pointing behind him, pointing towards the children. A chill crept across Remmy's spine. He had heard people use the expression of feeling like someone had stepped over their grave, but had never felt it himself. He did now.

Forcing himself to turn back towards the box, towards Tam and the three children, Remmy saw that the children had broken into a loping sprint, still on all fours, but were quickly closing the distance.

The lead child, a young boy, let out a high-pitched howl and that was when Remmy saw his teeth, both rows of them set in blood red gums like tiny bone daggers.

Remmy snatched the club from the ground with trembling hands, widened his stance and prepared to face the three Red children that bore down upon him like a pack of rabid wolves.

The Reds erupted into screams and laughs, as bets and predictions were made on the sides of the arena.

-36-

Captain Ortiz and his men stood shoulder to shoulder. A perfect line, all silent and expressionless, even their breathing was barely perceptible. Eldritch momentarily found himself wondering if he would actually have to give the men the command to breathe.

Moments before, screams filled the room as Ortiz and his soldiers writhed on the floor, grasping at the invisible force that assailed their heads. Eldritch had dialed back the frequency's strength from what he had used on his aide, ever so slightly, but kept it strong enough to ensure subservience.

What stood before Eldritch was a contingent of the ERC's most highly trained soldiers, who were now conveniently one hundred percent loyal to him. Concerns regarding Ortiz's own motivations and possible betrayal vanished with the clicks of a few keys. Eldritch couldn't help but marvel at the genius of his father's invention, but sneered at his short sightedness. How had he failed so miserably at attaining power and bringing the masses in line? The answer had been right in front of him the entire time. Was it a lack of vision or even worse, fear that kept his father from realizing the true potential of the Em-Pak? Either was inexcusable as far as Eldritch was concerned.

"Sir?" Captain Ortiz asked, shaking Eldritch from his thoughts.

"Yes? What is it, Captain?" Eldritch grumbled. Maybe he should increase Ortiz's signal. Thoughts of his aide's concave skull quickly dispersed such inklings.

"What are your orders, Mr. Eldritch, sir?" Ortiz asked, not from a sense of impatience, but rather from a newly seeded desire to serve without question.

"Ah, yes," Eldritch grinned. His Em-Pak chirped loudly. "Plans? Hmm, well, Captain, I think it's time we became a bit more proactive in our approach."

"Proactive, sir?" Ortiz asked. "Would you like us to continue the counterfeit Emo terrorist attacks? Maybe increase their frequency?" Eldritch smiled ever so slightly. It was good that Ortiz was asking questions. That meant that he still retained some of his ability to think, and be an effective captain, but not enough to lead to any problems.

"No, Captain," Eldritch shook his head. "I don't think there will be any need to continue those activities. The citizens have been made fully aware of the threat posed by the Reds and Emos. What little resistance to my leadership there was has been neutralized and my power is now absolute. What we need to do now is give the citizens something to do, something to aim them at if you will."

"Such as, sir?" Ortiz questioned.

"Such as the eradication of all threats," Eldritch explained. "The citizens have enjoyed safety and that has made them soft. It's time they began to give back to those who have protected them. I think it's time for a draft."

"A draft, sir?" Ortiz responded. "I beg your pardon, Mr. Eldritch, but at this time, there are more than sufficient ranks within the ERC troops. Why institute a draft, sir?"

Eldritch thought for a moment, pretending that he had to consider his plan, even though there was really no need to. He could tell Ortiz and his men that his plan was to dress in bunny costumes and throw marshmallows at schoolchildren and compliance would be assured. Perhaps this was simply a habit left from a time where emotions and motives mattered.

"The citizens need to feel that they play a role," Eldritch finally answered. "They need to feel that they have a hand in shaping their future. More importantly, they need to feel that they have something to lose. I need to ensure that I have the absolute support of the next generation, so what better way to do so than to bolster our ranks and wage a war against the Emos and Reds? It's due time that we took the fight outside our city walls, and that we take it to them."

"Understood, sir," Ortiz nodded. "Should I ready the ERC recruitment centers to assist in your efforts, sir? Perhaps have them draw up a list of the most eligible candidates?"

"That won't be necessary, Captain," Eldritch answered. "I have already compiled a list of the candidates I would like from powerful families."

"Powerful families, sir?" Ortiz asked. "With all due respect, Mr. Eldritch, the lower classes have greater numbers and more suitable dispositions, sir. Would it not make more sense to draw from there?"

"Eventually, Captain, yes it will," Eldritch agreed. "But what we're looking for now is support, and what better way to ensure that those who matter fall in line than to win over their children? By enlisting the privileged children, we all but ensure the support of their families."

"But, sir, why bother?" Ortiz asked.

"What do you mean, Captain?" Eldritch snapped.

"Couldn't you just activate their Em-Paks in a similar fashion to ours, sir?" Ortiz asked. Eldritch didn't like that the Captain was aware of what had been done to him and his men, but figured that it really didn't matter what he knew so long as he was subservient.

"Yes," Eldritch answered. "I guess I could, but where's the challenge in that, Captain? That simply wouldn't be fun."

Samuel led the way through the woods, using his small wrist computer to guide them towards the Red camp.

"Does anyone else think it's stupid that we're actually walking towards the Reds?" Xander complained from the rear of the line.

"Do you honestly think that we care about what you think?" Cora growled over her shoulder.

"Xander," Samuel said calmly, "there's many things about life that make a lot more sense once your Em-Pak is removed."

"Oh, I bet," Xander laughed sarcastically. "Because once you don't have an Em-Pak your life is considerably shorter."

"And yet here I am," Samuel shrugged, unfazed by his grandson's nastiness.

"About that," Xander began. "How come you never tried to come back to the cities? Sure, you can claim that the ERC would kill you, but if citizens saw you, they would side with you. You're like a god to most citizens."

"Perhaps," Samuel mused, "but it was too risky. The citizens have become reliant upon Em-Paks and the ERC. Anything threatening that would be destroyed, even me. Just because they bow to my picture does not mean that they would still love the man."

"Um, okay," Xander grunted and fell silent.

"Samuel," Cora asked, suddenly interested in the conversation. "I hate to say this, but Xander does have a point. How come you never tried to reach us? We're your family."

"I did," Samuel said. A cloud of sadness passed over his eyes. "I really did try to find a way, but the ERC monitors everything. All my attempts were dead ends. It was frustrating, but all I could do was keep tabs on you through the school computers. Contacting you would have exposed me to the ERC and possibly put you and Xander at risk."

"What about our father?" Cora asked. "Did they tell him you were alive?"

"No," Samuel shook his head. "My son believes that I am dead, but I'm not sure that knowledge of my continued existence would have made much of a difference to him. Sam was always such a driven boy, so focused. Now I see that those characteristics were his undoing. I once admired my boy for being able to ignore those things that didn't seem to matter, and focus completely on what he wanted, but now I see how that and his Em-Pak made him weak."

"Weak?" Xander snapped. "I can't believe that you would actually call him weak. Look at you, old man. You're nothing, an outlaw. A ghost at best. Who are you to judge my father? My father is a great man."

"But is he a great father?" Samuel retorted.

"His greatness is judged by his deeds, not his children," Xander argued. "Who cares about what kind of father he is."

"He should have," Cora added.

"Oh, shut up," Xander waved dismissively. "You are completely insufferable since your Em-Pak was removed."

"She's right, Xander," Samuel said, stopping on the trail. "Every man should be judged by his children. All of a man's accomplishments pale compared to how he raises his children. Being a parent is the most important thing a person can ever undertake. I only wish I had done better."

Xander made a rude noise. "Please. The two of you are ridiculous. How can you not see the importance in what our father did? He was insuring the future, making sure that we had a future."

"No," Cora answered. "He was making sure that *I* had a future, Xander. I was the one that father was grooming to enter politics to ultimately head the ERC. When did he ever do anything for your future? You were a Plan-B at best."

"Shut up, Cora!" Xander's voice lost its ferocity as his Em-Pak pinged loudly, erasing his anger. "Father had plans for me. He would have been able to focus on them more if you weren't such a problem, such a disappointment."

"I'd gladly disappoint him and his plans," Cora smiled. "I want nothing to do with his plans for my life. Father was, and still is, a monster."

Xander's hands shot forward and shoved his sister. Cora stumbled a few steps forward, but Samuel caught her and steadied her.

"Enough," Samuel said calmly, but firmly.

"Oh, no it's not," Cora grinned, a look of anger flaring in her eyes. "This has been coming for a long time. I'm sick of Xander's tantrums. It's time for baby to have *a time out.*" Cora lunged forward, striking Xander in the face. He tumbled to the ground in a cloud of red dust.

Xander coughed, the dust filling his lungs.

"Get up," Cora growled. "Get up right now!"

Xander coughed a few more times, playing up the impact of the dust while grabbing a handful of it from the path. He sprang to his feet, throwing the dirt into Cora's eyes before he dove forward, driving his head into her gut.

Cora grunted loudly and fell to the ground where Xander pinned her shoulders beneath his knees. Cora's eyes were wild and angry. Xander's were empty and cold.

"I said enough!" Samuel shouted as he pulled the two siblings apart. Cora snarled and lunged at Xander, but Samuel had her firmly by the collar of her jacket. Xander stood rail straight, a look of equal parts disdain and indifference etched into his dirty face.

Cora opened her mouth to shout something unkind, and continue the fight, because it had felt good, felt justified, but the sound of leaves rustling under foot and the dry snap of a branch silenced her. All three stood still listening to the sounds of the forest.

A Red sprang from the nearby bushes. It was a boy, not much older than Cora was, but his face was twisted into a mask of rage and feral hunger. Row upon row of pointed teeth gnashed together as the boy loped forward. He stood slightly stooped, a rusted hatchet held in his right hand, his left empty, but tipped in wickedly sharp nails.

"Samuel?" Cora whispered.

"Get behind me," Samuel said through his teeth. He released Cora and Xander, who did as their grandfather commanded. A look of deep sadness was in Samuel's eyes.

Cora was worried. Worried about the Red and if there were more, but more concerned about how her elderly grandfather was going to handle the Red. There was no way Samuel could win against the boy in a fight. Samuel was old and walked with a slight limp. The Red was young; his body was lean and muscled, trembling with the promise of violence.

The Red leapt forward, hatchet raised high overhead, a feral scream rumbling from his young throat. Samuel barely moved, just shifting his weight and bringing his right arm forward. He held his arm straight, his hand flexed and fingers splayed and pointing upward. A loud hiss filled the air as a small cloud burst from Samuel's jacket sleeve. The Red howled in pain. He stopped midair, as if colliding with some unseen wall and collapsed to the ground in a tangled heap.

Samuel slowly walked forward and checked the Red. He wasn't moving. The boy was dead.

"Come on," Samuel said, a look of remorse upon his face. "We need to get moving before more Reds show up. The noise will draw more."

"What did you do?" Cora gasped as she stepped forward to look at the Red. Countless tiny holes riddled his body and face like ruby freckles, each trailing its own thin, crooked line of blood.

Samuel slid back the sleeve of his jacket, revealing a small cylindrical container. Four black nylon straps held it in place on his wrist and forearm. A small lever was on the front of the canister, just within the reach of Samuel's thumb, but far enough back that no one would see it within his sleeve. "A simple device, really nothing more than small metal BB's packed together in front of a small container of compressed gas. When I pull the lever, it punctures the air canister and launches the BB's. Very similar to a shotgun, but silent," Samuel said as he turned his wrist over, exposing the weapon. He ejected the empty air canister, loaded another and refilled the BB's. "I take no pleasure in having invented it and even less in having to use it, but I will do whatever is required to keep you children safe and save your friend." Two more of the weapons were in Samuel's bag, but he prolonged giving them to his grandchildren, worrying about arming them and feeling guilty for having to do so.

"Why feel sorry for this...this *thing*?" Xander asked as he toed the body of the Red. "It was going to kill us and you killed it first. There's no shame in that."

"He was a boy, Xander," Cora replied. "Not much older than you or me. It could have been you or me!"

"I could have been *you*. I have an Em-Pak, so it's never going to be me," Xander shrugged as he kicked some dust onto the Red's body. "It was a Red, that's all. Samuel simply put down a rabid animal. There's no reason to feel remorseful over that."

"I'm sad because he was a child," Samuel replied, his words strained and raw. "And if the Em-Paks had been used properly, he probably would still be alive. His death, countless deaths are on my hands."

"But it's the ERC's fault, Samuel," Cora protested, but he waved his hand and continued down the path. It was clear that Samuel had already convicted himself of countless murders.

Cora watched the weight of Samuel's words press down upon him. Most days, he seemed so at peace, but now she could see the internal battle that was silently plaguing her grandfather, slowly killing him. Cora suddenly found herself worrying that maybe Samuel had accompanied them for reasons beyond the rescue of Remmy.

"Here," Samuel offered, looking even sadder, if that were possible. He held out two of the guns. One for Xander. One for Cora. "And this is perhaps the part I enjoy the least, but you need to be safe. I am just saddened by the fact that my grandchildren have to exist in a world where weapons are required to keep them safe, a world that I helped create."

-38-

The lead Red child, a little boy, leapt from the dusty, trampled ground. Remmy instinctively swung his arm up to stop the boy from burying his razor-like teeth in his neck, but screamed in agony as the flesh of his arm shredded between the Red's powerful jaws and sharp teeth. Remmy's screams were lost beneath the joyful cheers and taunts of the surrounding Reds.

The Red snarled and clamped its tiny jaws down harder onto Remmy's arm. Blood pooled around the edges of his lips before trailing off the sides. The boy snarled, causing the blood to burble and froth around his mouth.

"Get off! Get off!" Remmy screamed as he felt the Red's slender neck twist from one side to the other in an attempt to flay flesh from the bone. Pain made Remmy's head swim, but he refused to give in, controlled his breathing and demanded that his mind focus. There were still two more Reds to worry about.

Taking a deep breath, Remmy prepared himself to do what he needed to. He didn't want to hurt these children, even if they were Reds and trying to kill him, but he would need to do something. Remmy jammed the tapered end of the club into an open corner of the young Red's mouth. The tiny teeth bore into the tough wood. Remmy twisted the club sideways creating space and loosening the Red's grip. Feeling the vicious bite lessen a tiny bit, Remmy spun his arm, allowing the Red's body weight to pull him away. The child's bite finally broke and his small frame was sent pin wheeling across the arena where it collided with the side of one of the rusted buses. A loud *thunk* echoed off the side of the bus as the Red's small head smashed into the side. The boy fell to the ground and didn't get up. The crowd erupted with cheers. Remmy was happy the Red was off his arm, no longer tearing into his flesh, but still found himself hoping that the child had only been knocked unconscious, not killed.

The remaining Red children came at Remmy as a pair. He prepared to face them, but at the last minute, they split from one another, coming around from Remmy's sides. The two children launched themselves, jaws wide, for the back of Remmy's legs – they were going tear out the back of his knees and cripple him.

There was only time to deal with one of the Reds. Remmy chose the larger of the two, a girl, maybe eight years old at the most. Dropping his shoulder and swinging the club in a powerful upward arc, Remmy connected with the girl's chin. He felt the vibrations of his attack reverberate through the length of the club. His stomach churned, revolted by what he had just done.

The girl tumbled to the ground. A loud, bloody hack gurgled from the back of her throat as she spat shards of broken teeth onto the ground. She tried to right herself, but listed to the side and fell over. Remmy's attack had shaken her, but she would be back in the fight soon enough.

The last Red, a filthy wiry boy, who was so grimy Remmy couldn't even begin to predict his age, crashed into the side of Remmy's leg with the force of a small truck. Remmy's leg buckled underneath his weight and he fell to the ground. The Red clambered up Remmy's body, stopping at his stomach.

A wicked smirk spread across the boy's face as he reared his head back, exposing teeth that belonged in the mouth of a sea dwelling nightmare, not a child. The soft flesh of Remmy's stomach beckoned to the Red, calling for him to split it wide and peel it from Remmy's ribs.

Remmy rolled sideways. The Red lost his grip and tumbled with Remmy's rolling body. Remmy suddenly found himself pinning the boy to the ground with no idea of what to do next.

"Kill him!" someone shrieked from the edge of the arena. Remmy figured they were calling for his death, but as he looked up, he saw that it was Jessica. Jessica was screaming for Remmy to kill the boy. "Do it Remmy! Do it!" Hatch sat beside Jessica, a bemused smile on her face, but no real reaction to the events unfolding before her.

The young Red thrashed wildly under Remmy's grip. The blood from Remmy's bite wound spattered across the boy's dirty face, adding to the streaks of red paint that peeked out from underneath grime. The Red's teeth clacked together with bone rattling force. Remmy had to fight the urge to jump back each time the boy's teeth connected with the other rows.

The Reds on the edges of the arena began to grow bored. Screams and jeers were launched from the sides. Some threatened to join in, to finish what the children couldn't. Remmy glanced to the sides, were they really going to enter the arena? Was that allowed? Allowed? Remmy almost laughed. There were no rules. The Reds could do whatever they wanted.

Dropping his bloodied forearm onto the young Red's slender neck, Remmy pushed down, pressing against his windpipe and cutting off his air. The child might be a monster, but he still needed to breathe and Remmy was going to take that from him.

The Red thrashed with a renewed vigor as he felt his air supply being cut off. His eyes bulged and thin tendrils of blood began to curl towards his dilated pupils from the corners of his eyes. The child stopped moving.

Remmy jumped to his feet, remembering that the girl was still a threat, but she had collapsed to the ground, evidently crumbling under the violence of Remmy's attack. Remmy had won. He felt relieved to be alive. He felt completely disgusted with himself. But he didn't feel angry.

"Did you get what you wanted?" Remmy shouted as he eyed the other Reds. He had won, but he hadn't changed. Remmy could only think of one way he was getting out of the arena – on dinner plates. "Are we done? Let's get this over with!"

"Done?" a gruff voice barked, the words sounding as if they were dragged across sandpaper and shards of glass. "Oh, no food," Tam grinned, "we aren't done at all." He pulled a wicked looking axe from behind his back and spun it at his side.

"Tam!" a wild voice commanded. Notes of something wild, yet feminine painted the words with strange tones. Remmy could hear that the voice had once been beautiful, something made for songs, the kind of voice that could lull children to sleep simply through words, foregoing the trickery of nursery rhymes. Now it spoke of nothing but violence and pain.

Tam froze in his tracks, the axe held at half ready. Hatch had risen from her seat causing the other Reds to become silent. "What are you doing, Tam? The boy won. You know the rules!"

"He hasn't changed," Tam protested, "hasn't become one of us. He's food."

"He won, Tam!" Hatch growled. Remmy was surprised to see Tam actually step back a few steps, startled by the ferocity in Hatch's voice.

"I have the right to redeem myself," Tam yelled, though with slightly less force than before. He pointed to his crooked, bruised nose. "I have a right to challenge him."

Hatch paused for a moment mulling over what Tam had said. What Remmy didn't realize is that there were rules and Hatch, being the chief, was responsible for interrupting them as she saw fit.

Jessica leapt up and tapped Hatch on the shoulder. Her eyes gleamed with mischief. She whispered something into Hatch's ear that spread a wide toothy grin across both of their faces. Remmy found no comfort in Jessica's intercession.

"Fine," Hatch snapped. "You do have the right to redeem yourself. That is the rule." Tam smiled as he eyed down Remmy. "But you also know that if this boy beats you that he takes your place. That is also the rule."

"Take my place?" Tam laughed. "He's not one of us!" Remmy could hear a handful of other Reds rumbling on the edges of the arena.

"Shut your mouth, Tam! Those are the rules! You knew that when you challenged him," Hatch barked. The Reds fell silent. "If this boy plans on living much longer, he had better be one of us by the end of the fight."

-39-

"Evolution of all things is an inevitability, a rule of nature, even with regards to our way of life. The ERC Council kept you safe, kept you sheltered from the storm that raged outside of our cities' walls. Their approach worked for some time, but became stagnant and it is that lack of action that led to their unfortunate downfall.

But fear not citizens, their fate does not determine ours! No! Our future is bright my fellow citizens, as long as we are willing to take the action required to ensure that it is! For it is action that is demanded in these troubling moments! We must take up arms against those that threaten our cities, threaten our way of life.

It is time we did more than just defend ourselves from the vicious Reds and traitorous Emos! It is time we took the fight to them! But our brave ERC soldiers alone cannot fight the battle that looms on the horizon. No, my fellow citizens, we must all join in the fight and shed blood, both theirs and ours, to ensure that our future is bright. That is the cost. That is the price to be paid.

I am immediately instituting a draft to bolster our ranks and ensure our success. I know that these words, these actions must be as disconcerting for you as they are for me, but I promise you one thing my fellow citizens, and that is success, but only through these means will it be achieved. Were there another method I would gladly employ it, but I have weighed the options and this is all that remains. To deviate from this path will lead us to only one end, death. The decision was mine my fellow citizens, but the choice is yours. Life or death."

Eldritch listened to his words replayed throughout the city on the same speakers that had once broadcast the ERC Council's message of compliance. He knew that his words were essentially the same thing, really nothing more than some overly dramatic words to get the cattle to move in the right direction. Eldritch was satisfied with his words, even if they were a little over the top. With Em-Paks, there really was no need for overly emotional statements and speeches, but in the end, Eldritch was still a

135

politician and some habits simply refused to be lost beneath the influence of an Em-Pak.

The citizens had responded well, offering up their youth, but few came from the more privileged families. Eldritch would gladly take the lower class, use them as cannon fodder, but ensuring his complete control meant holding the lives of those rich, undeserving little snots in the palm of his hand. The rich did what they always did and tried to resist, tried to find some means of excluding their children from the draft. Surely there was an extra tax that could be paid or possibly a stand in could be provided, fairly compensated of course.

Eldritch demanded that they enter the draft, even if it was little more than a puppet show. He knew full well what numbers would be drawn, had programmed the computers to select children from the most politically connected families. When he met with resistance, Eldritch simply turned off one or two family members' Em-Paks, unleashing a Red or two within the immaculate halls of mansions and high-rise apartments. No one was safe. No one could hide. Eldritch made sure that point was clear.

Eventually, all of the citizens, even the rich and powerful, fell in line. The ranks of the ERC army swelled with the bodies of children who had lived on little more than their last names and trust funds. Eldritch had complete control.

"Mr. Eldritch, sir?" Captain Ortiz asked as he walked into the immense office that had previously been the ERC Council's chambers. Eldritch stood in front of the massive window looking out over the Stele, his city. All of the cities were his city.

"Remember when we first took control of this office, Captain Ortiz?" Eldritch asked, still looking out the window. The sunset in the distance, splashing brilliant hues across the sky that neither man had the ability or inclination to appreciate.

"Yes sir," Ortiz nodded, "I do, sir."

"Remember how you worried about my desk being in front of this window?" Eldritch continued.

"I do, sir," Ortiz answered. "I was concerned about an attempt being made on your life. It was not a good idea to have you positioned in such an open area on a daily basis. With all due respect, Mr. Eldritch, sir, I still don't think it is a wise decision, even with the bullet proof glass installed."

Eldritch waved his hand dismissively. "Ortiz, there is not a citizen in any city that would stand against me now. To control the youth is to control the future. No citizen is stupid enough to challenge me when their child's life rests squarely in the palm of my hand."

"Sir?" Ortiz questioned. "Is it wise to rely upon out of date constructs like family, loyalty and love? These motivations have all become extinct with the implantation of Em-Paks."

"Love?" Eldritch snorted. "I'm not putting any stock in anyone's love for their children. Who the hell *loves* their children? God lord, does anyone even use that term anymore? Honestly, Ortiz, I'm shocked you'd even think I'd make such a mistake."

"My apologies, sir," Ortiz responded. "Perhaps I require some clarification. Of course, only as long as it is acceptable for me to ask for it, sir."

"Yes, of course," Eldritch said slowly. He had Ortiz and his men under his control, but he still knew better than to trust them completely. "My point was, Captain, that every citizen, especially those rich and powerful ones, are concerned with ensuring their legacy, which could be viewed as their wealth, possessions or work, but ultimately everyone's ability to live forever is realized through their children. By taking control of these citizens' children I have essentially taken away their future and legacy."

"Understood sir," Ortiz nodded. "Their loyalty will determine whether or not they have any hope of regaining control over their legacies."

"Exactly," Eldritch grinned. "As I said in my speech, the choice is theirs to make. Life or death, it's really that simple, Ortiz."

"Yes, sir," Ortiz agreed. "Quite clear."

"Glad you agree, Ortiz," Eldritch joked sarcastically, even though his sense of humor was suppressed by his Em-Pak. "Your astute observations and unbiased opinions have always been your most admirable qualities."

"Thank you sir," Ortiz said flatly.

"Are the troops ready?" Eldritch asked, growing bored and changing the subject.

"Almost all of those who were called into service by the draft have reported to local ERC stations," Ortiz reported. "There are still a few that are being somewhat reluctant, sir. I have compiled a list of those names for you, Mr. Eldritch, so that they can be compelled to comply. I will have all of the new recruits prepared for service within the next few days. The new Em-Pak programs have streamlined training and eliminated the need for an extended boot camp."

"Excellent," Eldritch nodded. "I want them ready to go in two days, Captain. That is all." Eldritch held out his hand for the list of families that had resisted enlisting their children.

"Understood sir," Ortiz answered. He handed Eldritch the list and turned to attend to his orders.

Eldritch collapsed into his studded leather desk chair. He punched the Em-Pak ID numbers into his computer, sentencing the corresponding people to death without so much as a long look at the screen.

"I made it clear to them," Eldritch mumbled. If these citizens were still too strong willed then they faced the same fate as the ERC Council. People needed to grow, to find a new place within his vision of society. Those that clung to the old ways were useless. Eldritch wondered how many more examples he would have to make before the citizens realized their place – probably not too many more.

"Time will tell," Eldritch shrugged, answering his own question. He powered down his computer and got up from his desk. He had done enough for today. He was exhausted and it was time for some well-deserved rest.

Eldritch flicked off the lights and locked his office. In his tired state, he failed to realize that he had left his phone on the desk, a phone that now lit up and vibrated as it received an SOS signal relayed to his phone from an ERC emergency radio transmitter – a radio transmitter that was supposed to have been lost in the wreckage of his family's limo accident.

-40-

"Eat something," Samuel said holding out a grizzled stick of jerky to Xander. They had brought other supplies, but making a fire was too risky after the run in with the young Red.

"I don't want that garbage," Xander grunted as he pushed away his grandfather's hand.

"You've haven't eaten anything since we left camp and from what I was told, very little even before that," Samuel continued.

"I'm not going to put that crap into my body," Xander sneered. "Who knows what the hell is even in there? It's probably road kill."

"Suit yourself," Cora smiled and snatched the jerky from Samuel.

"Figures you'd eat it," Xander grinned without an ounce of humor. "You've gone native, become a full blown savage. You'll probably be eating bugs and painting on cave walls by the end of the night."

"You've got bugs?" Cora teased. "Now I'm really hunger. Why'd you have to go and talk about bugs?" Teasing Xander seemed to come naturally to Cora.

Xander made a rude noise and snatched a second piece of jerky that Samuel held out.

"Thank you," Samuel said to Xander.

"Save it," Xander grunted and turned his back on Samuel and Cora. Soon they would be asleep and then Xander could check the signal on his radio transmitter. It had been a few hours since he pretended to scratch his leg and flicked the homing signal button. Xander hoped that he was far enough out of the dense woods that it would be picked up by the ERC and sent to his father, but he had no way of knowing. Ideally, Xander would have liked to have waited for a clearing, but he had to keep the transmitter hidden and time was running out. Samuel estimated that they would be near the Red camp by tomorrow night.

Samuel checked the small screen on his wrist. Small red dots merged into crooked lines that eventually connected to larger masses, spreading across the screen like a bloody amoeba. Samuel had known the Reds were coming together, joining up for a reason known only to them, but even he was shocked by what he saw on the small screen. He would seriously need to reconsider their plan. It had at first seemed feasible to cause a distraction that would allow Cora to slip in and rescue Remmy, but now that plan was little more than a death sentence for his granddaughter.

"We need a new plan, right?" Cora asked from where she looked over Samuel's shoulder. He hadn't even noticed her presence.

"So it would seem," Samuel admitted. There was no reason to keep anything hidden from Cora, even the impossible odds that were stacking up against them. "There are more Reds than I had ever imagined. They must be coming from miles and miles away. I am really at a loss as to why."

"Doesn't matter," Cora replied. "I don't care if it's for a birthday party or a barbeque..." Her words trailed off as she thought about what she had just said. A *barbeque*. Samuel told her that he believed the Reds to be cannibalistic, having found a few fragmented bones in the woods with teeth marks. Were the Reds coming together to eat Remmy? Cora felt sick and furious with herself. How could she even allow herself to say something like that? How could she have been so freaking stupid? Cora was happy to be free of her Em-Pak, allowed to feel things, like how she felt around Remmy, but the opposite end of the deal was excruciating. Self-doubt, guilt and disgust surged through Cora making her head light.

"It's okay," Samuel smiled weakly. "Members of the Eldritch family have always had the ability to move their mouths faster than their minds. Cora, I know what you meant to say and I'm sure that Remmy would have too. Beating yourself up for a slip of the tongue isn't going to do anyone any good."

"I guess so," Cora muttered without conviction. In her mind's eye, Remmy was lashed to a spit, slowly turning over a fire surrounded by slavering Reds. Doubt crept in, strangling Cora's hopes like weeds. Tears glistened in the corner of her eyes.

Xander quietly shook his head, disgusted at his sister's emotional display.

"Look here," Samuel said holding out his wrist for Cora to see. He had zoomed in on the main Red camp. A countless number of Reds formed a massive ring around three red dots and one yellow dot. The four dots moved as if dancing with one another. "Remmy's still alive."

"But what are they doing to him?" Cora demanded. "What's going on there?" She was relieved to see Remmy's yellow dot glowing vibrantly on the screen, moving and full of life, but the Red dots appeared to be trailing him or maybe even chasing him.

"I'm not sure, Cora," Samuel admitted. He sighed heavily and decided to be honest. "Cora, remember when I said that Remmy was alive because he fought back?"

"Yeah," Cora nodded. "He attacked that one Red. Hit him in the face with a rock. Why?"

"Well," Samuel paused. He needed to be honest. Deceit served no purpose. "I'm not one hundred percent sure, Cora, but from what I can surmise, I'd guess that the Reds are having Remmy prove himself again."

"Prove himself?" Cora questioned. "What do you mean?"

"He means fight, you moron," Xander chimed in. "A huge ring like that and four dots in the middle? Sure sounds like a gladiator arena to me. Boy, that's got to be a sight. All those Reds and your dirty little boy toy in the middle of it all."

Cora wanted to attack Xander, to claw his eyes, but there was no time to waste. Angry words died and festered in her throat.

Samuel cut in before Xander could say more. "I think it would be a good idea if we kept moving. We can sleep when we're done saving Remmy, right?"

"You mean, we can sleep when we're dead," Xander added humorlessly and climbed to his feet. He spat the half-chewed wad of jerky onto the ground and began walking.

-41-

Remmy was granted a brief rest following his fight with the Red children. Hatch demanded that he be fresh for his fight with Tam. She didn't want anyone complaining about unfair fights, but Remmy suspected it had more to do with Jessica than a sense of fair play. Either way, Remmy greeted the respite with a mix of emotions. On one hand, he was glad to be out of the foul arena, but knew that he would soon be thrown back in to face something far worse than three Red children.

The dingy shack felt heavy, filled with the stagnant air of a tomb. Remmy forced himself to breathe, to get lungful after lungful of the charnel air. He needed to remain focused. Remmy had gotten the best of Tam before and that saved his life, but he doubted that Tam would make the same mistake twice. Rage burned brightly in Tam's eyes as he glared at Remmy from across the arena. The fact that Remmy had injured Tam called into question the man's position as second in command. There was no question that Tam was a vicious warrior, and few wanted to challenge that, but a human, a boy at that, not even a full-grown man, had bested him. That fact couldn't be ignored. Tam was going make sure there were no questions remaining at the end of the fight.

Remmy grabbed a strip of filthy fabric from the pile in the corner of the shack. He had to wrap his wound and make sure that a slick of blood didn't interfere with his ability to fight. The rag was disgusting, covered in countless germs, but Remmy doubted he'd live long enough for the bite to become infected.

"Get that look off your face!" Jessica snapped from the doorway. Remmy looked past her and watched the sun drop lower in the sky. Night was coming and soon he would be forced back into the arena. Memories of time spent in the fields, some even with Jessica, flooded Remmy's head. Would this be the last sunset he would ever see? The last time he would ever watch the brilliant colors of a dying day stretch across an indigo sky? He would miss these colors. He already missed Cora.

"What look?" Remmy grunted and turned his back on Jessica. Before he could turn completely away, Jessica dashed across the shack with incredible speed. She snapped her teeth savagely mere inches from Remmy's face. His hands shot out instinctively to push Jessica away from him.

"Good. Very good," Jessica said through her shark-like grin. "You've still got some fight in you. You're going to need that against Tam."

"What I need is a freaking tank," Remmy spat. "He's a monster. You all are." Remmy added the last bit in an attempt to hurt Jessica. The toothy smile never once flickered. If his words cut Jessica she refused to show it.

"A tank would help," Jessica shrugged, "but I wouldn't count on it. You need to find some way to beat him."

"And how's that going to happen?" Remmy demanded. "He's going to gut me in front of all you and for what? Because of some rule made up by Hatch?"

"The rules are NOT made up!" Jessica growled. "The rules are what keep order! The rules are what kept you alive, Remmy! So I wouldn't be so quick to write off the rules or Hatch for that matter. Besides me, Hatch is the only friend you've got right now!" A devious look fell over Jessica's red painted face. She knew something that she wasn't telling Remmy. Some secret was being withheld.

"Hatch, my friend?" Remmy sneered. "Jeez, well if that's true then Tam must want to hug me to death. What the hell are you talking about, Jessica?"

"Look," Jessica whispered, her words slurred by row upon row of dagger-like teeth. "Hatch knows that Tam wants her spot and so far she's been able to keep him in line, but that's not going to last forever. You smashing Tam's face made the others question his ability to lead."

"So what?" Remmy replied. "Like I care about some Red power play. It doesn't matter who's the king of your dirty little ant hill, I'm dead either way."

"Not necessarily," Jessica grinned, her teeth too large for her mouth. "Hatch wants Tam gone. You do that and you're free."

"Free to be a Red you mean?" Remmy scoffed. "Hatch said it herself that I had better be a Red by the end of the fight if I wanted to live."

"Free is free," Jessica replied. "Hatch will keep her word. If you kill Tam, his spot is yours."

"As long as I'm infected," Remmy growled.

"Infected, evolved, whatever. Who cares?" Jessica said. "However you look at it, at least you're alive. Dead and self-righteous is still dead."

"Why the hell do you even care?" Remmy demanded. "And don't feed me any of that crap about being my friend. You and I both know that's a total load. What are you getting out of this?"

The smile faded from Jessica's face, her lips struggling to conceal her pointed teeth. She sat back and crossed her legs, her eyes level with Remmy's own. "The truth?"

"That would be nice," Remmy said, a fake smile wrinkling his face.

"The truth is that I hate Tam," Jessica answered.

"I'm sure a lot people feel that way," Remmy replied. "Please, I'm sure a lot Reds probably feel that way."

"Yeah," Jessica said softly, "but none of them are promised to Tam."

"Promised?" Remmy asked. "You mean for like marriage or something?"

"Every king needs a queen I guess," Jessica grunted. "He won me, so I'm his unless someone else takes his place."

"So whoever is second in command owns you?" Remmy asked. "Can't Hatch do anything? Why can't she just kill him?"

"No she can't do anything," Jessica sighed. "Hatch doesn't like it anymore than I do, but if she challenges Tam and kills him, then the rules say she took his place, which means no one is left to lead. It would create chaos, everyone struggling to take control. The rules say Hatch can't step down, only be taken down and replaced. The leader of the Reds is never allowed to retire, only die. Tam is dumb, but even he's not stupid enough to challenge Hatch in the arena."

"Those rules are stupid," Remmy added. "She's the leader. She can do what she wants."

"Not really," Jessica replied. "Sure, being the leader has its benefits, but it's a shaky throne that Hatch sits on. She always has to worry about someone trying to kill her. Worry about the rules."

"Enough with these stupid freaking rules!" Remmy shouted. "Why are they so important? No offense, but I really don't see much going on around here that needs rules."

"That's exactly the point," Jessica answered. "You don't see things going on around here. The rules are what keep us from destroying each other. If there were no rules the Reds would turn on each other. Hatch and her rules are the only thing that keep our people safe."

"Your people?" Remmy snorted. "Your people were back in the camp, Jessica, not here. You're not a person."

"So kind of you to notice," Jessica said sarcastically. "Save your judgments, Remmy. The Reds are my people now. None of us asked for what we've become, so how can we be condemned for it? We're only doing what every other person is trying to do – survive. Why is that so wrong?"

"It's not," Remmy replied. "But how you survive is. Kidnapping people, forcing them to become Reds or eating them if they don't. It's disgusting."

"You think I want to eat people?" Jessica asked. "You think that was something I thought about before I changed?"

"How the hell should I know?" Remmy answered, but a note of sadness in Jessica's voice pierced Remmy's heart. Jessica had been exactly where he was, had been given the exact same odds. She hadn't asked for any of this. "I'm sorry. I guess not."

"Of course not," Jessica continued, "but what are we supposed to do? That is what my body demands. We eat other things, but if we don't at least eat some people then we begin to break down, turn back into screaming monsters."

"So eating people is what keeps you from turning back?" Remmy asked.

"Exactly," Jessica smiled. "Isn't it better that we eat a few instead of being some mindless monster that kills without reason or thought? It's nature, Remmy. We don't want to kill all people, just enough to survive."

"Sure," Remmy snapped. "Don't want to mess up the food supply."

"You know, I don't remember you being so whiny," Jessica teased, clacking her teeth together. "I'm getting a little sick of your prejudice, Remmy."

Remmy let out an acerbic laugh. "But you need my help."

"And you need mine," Jessica added. "I know how you can beat Tam. He's tough, but I know something most people don't."

"And if I do beat him," Remmy paused, "then what?"

"You take his place," Jessica answered, "assuming you've changed."

"But you said whoever takes his place owns you," Remmy continued. "That would mean that –"

"That we'd be together," Jessica said, finishing Remmy's sentence. "I'd much rather be promised to you instead of Tam." Jessica paused and then added, "Even if you are whiny."

"Fine," Remmy relented. "Tell me what to do." He listened intently as Jessica filled in the gaps in the plan. Remmy had a chance to beat Tam, albeit an extremely thin one, but it was better than nothing. As Jessica got up to leave, Remmy suddenly found himself not only worrying about the fight, but also what would happen after.

-42-

The Emo camps fell beneath the heavy booted feet of the ERC troops. Eldritch watched with as much joy as his Em-Pak allowed as an ERC trooper smashed the butt of his rifle into the face of a fleeing Emo. Another soldier held down a man while a second soldier repeatedly stabbed him in the stomach. The man screamed. Eldritch grinned for a fraction of a second before his Em-Pak chirped loudly. Sometimes, just sometimes, Eldritch mused, he would like to turn his Em-Pak off and enjoy the satisfaction of a job well done. His ERC troops, led by an obedient Captain Ortiz, had left four Emo camps as little more than smoldering piles of ash and bone. These images were exclusively for Eldritch's enjoyment, sent through a secure line, direct to his computer. The images released to the citizens were far more inflammatory, showing carefully edited scenes of ERC soldiers bravely battling Emo terrorists and monstrous Reds.

The Reds presented a slightly more irksome problem than the Emos. The Reds were moving, never staying in one area and this worried Eldritch and Ortiz. In the past, the Reds appeared to be somewhat territorial. They stayed within certain hunting grounds, but now there was large-scale movement of huge numbers of Reds. Ortiz had speculated that they were regrouping and perhaps joining together for some sort of organized attack, but Eldritch had dismissed the idea as idiotic. The Reds were incapable of coherent thought, let alone planning something of that magnitude.

"Sir?" Ortiz's voice called through the speakers of Eldritch's computer. "We're approaching the signal now, Mr. Eldritch. We should have contact within the minute."

Eldritch ordered Ortiz and his troops to track down the SOS signal being transmitted by the emergency radio linked to his family's limo. Of course, that had been after a few successful battles that could be fed to the slavering masses. Eldritch had to think of the people before himself, he was of course, a public servant. Besides, images of a rescue attempt would only serve to undermine the progress he had made enraging the masses. Allowing those flames to be cooled by whatever was at the end of that radio signal was foolish. If his wife or children were still alive, well that was acceptable, and surely could be spun into some sort of support for his cause. Furthermore, whoever had sent that signal had clearly survived this long, so what harm would a few more days do?

"Approach with caution, Captain," Eldritch ordered. He was beaming a live feed of the rescue through all media outlets accessible by citizens. An ERC reporter rode alongside Ortiz's troops to provide images and commentary.

"We're closing in, Mr. Eldritch," Ortiz reported. "There appears to be numerous heat signatures, possibly an Emo camp or group of Reds. Should we begin the live feed?"

"Yes," Eldritch commanded. "Make sure this goes smoothly, Captain."

"Understood, sir," Ortiz answered. "Beginning the feed now."

Eldritch pressed the button to turn on the large screen that hung on his wall. Dark woods rushed past the windows of Ortiz's vehicle. The ERC reporter allowed a few more seconds of footage before beginning her commentary.

"We wait with bated breath," the reporter began, "as we approach the signal being transmitted from the wreck that possibly claimed the lives of Assemblyman Eldritch's family. Surely, this will be a great moment for Assemblyman Eldritch and for all citizens, really. The brave ERC soldiers, led by Captain Ortiz, will either rescue a stranded member of the Eldritch family or punish those responsible for the attack that claimed their lives. We're closing in now."

The camera turned back to film through the windshield of Ortiz's vehicle. Branches scraped and slapped across the glass, obscuring the view. Suddenly, the woods broke and the vehicle rumbled into a large clearing.

Countless numbers of cows turned to stare at Ortiz's vehicle with oversized glassy eyes. A few loud moos could be heard over the throaty diesel roar of the vehicle's engine.

"Cut the feed!" Eldritch screamed. "Cut the feed right now, Captain!"

The last image transmitted was that of Ortiz's large, black-gloved hand covering the camera lens and pulling it down.

"Damn it! How the hell is that possible! Who is transmitting that signal?" Eldritch shouted at an empty office. His Em-Pak began desperately beeping, trying to control his anger. The entire rescue mission built up for days and fed to the idiotic masses, had been a failure, nothing more than some feral herd of cattle.

"Sir?" Ortiz's voice, tinny and electronic, rattled from the small computer speakers. "Orders on how to proceed, Mr. Eldritch?"

"Return, Captain," Eldritch snapped. "But find something to kill on the way back and make it look good, Ortiz. I don't care how many men you need to order to walk into Emo bullets or Red jaws, just give me something to make the memory of this disaster go away!"

"Understood sir," Ortiz answered.

-43-

"The Red camp is on the other side of this rise," Samuel said as he looked at his wrist screen. He, Cora, and Xander had walked most of the night and morning to get to the camp as soon as possible. "We need to wait until dusk before we make our move."

"Dusk?" Cora questioned, her voice desperate and raw. "How can we wait that long? Remmy might be dead by then."

"We can't do anything in the broad daylight, Cora," Samuel answered. "We'd be seen and killed. Staying hidden is the only way to tip the odds in our favor, even if it's just a little bit."

"But, Samuel," Cora began to protest.

"Waiting for dusk is best," Samuel said firmly. He paused to look down at the screen strapped to his wrist. Pressing a few buttons, he changed the image. This screen showed white dots moving slowly across the screen, but the background looked completely different. "Excellent," Samuel grinned. "Yes, dusk will give us the advantage we need."

"What is that?" Xander demanded. "What's on that screen?"

"Satellites," Samuel responded, "ERC military satellites to be exact."

"What the hell are you going to do with an ERC military satellite?" Xander snapped.

"That you'll have to wait for dusk to see, my grandson," Samuel smiled.

"Don't call me that!" Xander growled. "I may have been related to you at one point, but my grandfather is dead."

"Suit yourself," Samuel shrugged, appearing unfazed by Xander's hurtful words. Samuel knew that Xander was just trying to get a reaction, and start an argument, but he wasn't going to give him the satisfaction, no matter how painful his words were.

"I'm going to rest over here," Xander muttered as he walked towards a shady copse of trees. "I'm kind of tired since someone had me walking all night."

Cora sneered at Xander, but was happy to have him go away for a while.

"Oh, Xander, one thing before you go to have a nap," Samuel grinned, his eyes bright with playful mischief.

"What?" Xander grunted.

"That radio transmitter in your sock?" Samuel pointed to Xander's right leg. "Can I have it please?"

Cora felt a sense of deep satisfaction as she watched the color drain from her brother's face. She had no idea that Xander was carrying a radio, and was terrified to think about what he could have possibly done with it, but was relieved to hear that Samuel had known about it all along.

"What?" Xander gasped. His Em-Pak began beeping, barely a pause in between the tinny chimes. "How? How'd you...I don't...what? How? How the hell did you know?"

Samuel walked over and snatched the radio out of Xander's sock before he had a chance to smash it.

"Come now, Xander," Samuel smiled. "Whether or not you want to acknowledge that I'm your grandfather doesn't change the fact that I designed the majority of the ERC's technology, including the emergency radio transmitters in every ERC vehicle. And of course, you being my grandson, I assumed that you would find some opportunity to sneak back and retrieve it from the wreck. After all, you are an Eldritch, my boy."

"But I activated that..." Xander started say.

"Two days ago," Samuel cut in, completing his grandson's thought. "Yes, I was aware of that. The signal showed up on the screen. Tracking ERC signals is one of the best ways to avoid the ERC. Simply, common sense."

"But the ERC is coming for me," Xander said weakly. "I'm sure that they are. Father must have sent someone days ago."

"Oh, that he did," Samuel grinned, "but they won't find you. Not when I rerouted the SOS signal through seven different satellites and changed the coordinates. If my calculations are correct, which I'm guessing they were, then your ERC rescue team recovered something more bovine than boy."

"You bastard," Xander seethed. His Em-Pak chirped, erasing the look of rage that simmered in his eyes, but he still glared at Samuel. "Where did you send them?"

"To a cattle field," Samuel grinned. "Knowing your father, my son, I figured that he would make some sort of spectacle out of the rescue, trying to use it for political purposes, so I figured he needed a little bit of humbling."

"Bastard," Xander spat. "Now they'll never find me."

"On the contrary," Samuel shook his head. "The ERC will track this signal once again tonight. In fact, it will lead them directly here."

"What?" Cora gasped. "Samuel, that's suicide. We can't call the ERC officers down on ourselves. How is that going to help Remmy?"

"We're not calling them down on us," Samuel corrected Cora, "We're calling them down on the Reds. We'll be gone with Remmy before then, but I figure that between the ERC and what I plan to do with the satellites, the Reds will have more to worry about than an escaped prisoner."

Cora couldn't help but smile. Her grandfather was a genius. Success felt real, and almost possible, thanks to Samuel.

"And Xander," Samuel added, "if you want to hide here and then reveal yourself to the ERC, you may. The choice is yours, but returning with us means that I will have to remove your Em-Pak. As I said before, I won't make that choice for you nor will I prevent you from returning to your father if you feel that is the best decision. But please consider your choice carefully, Xander. There is so much good we could accomplish. I can see my spark in you, my grandson. The world has so much to offer you once your Em-Pak is gone. Please just think about it."

"Offer me once my Em-Pak is gone?" Xander repeated. "So much, huh? Like pain or death or possibly infection? Are those the things you're offering me, Samuel? Gee, what a gift to give your grandson. I think I'll pass."

"Fine," Cora snapped. "You made your choice. Now shut up and go take a nap!"

"Xander," Samuel called as his grandson walked away, "you need to think about what that life offers you. People need to be free to feel and choose as they see fit, even if it puts them at risk. It's no different than how life was before the virus and still humanity survived. But Em-Paks are wrong, Xander. They rob us of the very things that make us human. Please consider staying with us, your family. The ERC is wrong, always has been. Living with no emotions is not living at all. I won't allow that to continue. I can't allow the ERC to continue."

Samuel's face was firm and grim, but his eyes were sad. His words were not meant as a threat, rather a plea for his grandson to choose a different life, a full one. Nevertheless, Samuel would never force this upon Xander. He had already seen what forcing decisions upon people led to and that mistake was one that he never wanted to make again.

"I know who my family is," Xander snapped as he disappeared into the inky shadows beneath the trees.

"I'm sorry, Samuel," Cora said softly, her hand on her grandfather's shoulder.

"Me too, Cora. Me too," Samuel whispered as tears welled in the corners of his eyes. "But he has to choose for himself. Xander has to be free to decide his own fate, even if it is the wrong one."

-44-

"Be silent!" Hatch bellowed from atop one of the rusted hulking school buses. She was smaller than many of the other Reds, especially the men, but radiated an unspoken threat of violence that couldn't be matched by the others. Jessica told Remmy that Hatch was one of the first Reds to make it through the first phase of infection and that while she looked thin; Hatch was a vicious fighter who had built her kingdom upon the bones and blood of her enemies.

Remmy stood at one end of the arena, an axe loosely held in one hand. Dented, abandoned cars were scattered throughout the ring, stained with both blood and rust. Across the arena, Remmy could see Tam, his shoulders heaving and an axe clenched in one of his hammy fists. Remmy hoped that what Jessica told him was true.

"Tam, you have chosen to challenge this boy, Remmy," Hatch boomed over the arena. All other Reds sat silent as Hatch spoke. "You seek revenge for the injury dealt to you by Remmy during the raid. That is your right. Those are the rules."

"Damn right, they are!" Tam screamed, his eyes wide and swimming with insanity. Hatch glared at Tam, obviously angered by his interruption. Remmy could almost see the hatred that existed between the two. "The rules also state that in challenging another, you have put your position at risk. Should this boy win, he will take your place and all that goes along with it."

"I know the damn rules, Hatch!" Tam sneered.

"Then you must also be aware of the fact that should you lose, you will be eaten," Hatch smiled, her pointed teeth shining in the dying rays of a setting sun.

"That's never been a rule," Tam growled, "what are you talking about?"

"You saw fit to challenge this boy in the arena," Hatch grinned. "Death in the arena means food on the plate. That is also a rule, Tam. You knew that."

"That's a rule for humans, not Reds!" Tam shouted. "No Red has ever been eaten for losing a challenge."

"Challenges aren't usually fought in the arena either," Hatch glared, "but that was your choice, Tam, so the rules state that the loser will be food. Whoever dies, or can no longer fight, will be made ready for the table."

"Whatever," Tam snapped, "I'm not going to lose!" He swung the axe in front of him imagining its blade peeling Remmy's flesh.

"Remmy," Hatch shouted, "win and Tam's position and property are yours." Hatch motioned towards Jessica who sat beside her. "Fight well." Hatch waved her hand before settling back into her chair.

Before Remmy had completely turned his head, Tam was already halfway across the arena. Nothing stood between him and Tam aside from the rusted shell of a small car, half buried in the hard packed dirt.

"Time to die!" Tam screamed as he launched himself from the top of the wrecked car. The rusted roof buckled under his weight and force.

Remmy waited, as if frozen in place by fear, as Tam rocketed towards him like a missile. Tam pulled back his axe, preparing to bury it in the center of Remmy's skull.

The surrounding Reds screamed with excitement and jeers. They wanted blood, more importantly they wanted food, but not before a show. Was the boy really just going to give up and choose to die quickly? Hatch and Jessica remained silent, watching with interests that were fanned by the flames of wants far deeper than those of the other Reds. They needed Tam to die. If he won there was no stopping him and he'd come for Hatch next. Hatch didn't fear a fight with Tam, but knew the cost of winning would most likely leave her open for another challenger to claim victory. No, this way was smarter and safer.

Moments, before Tam brought his axe down, Remmy shifted his weight and shot out to the left. Tam continued forward, as if completely unaware of Remmy's movement. The blade of Tam's axe *thunked* loudly as it chewed into the hard ground where Remmy had only seconds ago stood.

Tam grunted loudly and bared his teeth as he wrenched the axe from the ground. In spite of the danger, Remmy smiled. Jessica had told him the truth.

Earlier, while Remmy waited for what he was sure would be his death, he had begun to wonder why Hatch would allow him a rest. Why hold off on the inevitable? Remmy figured that it had something to do with 'the rules' or simply a dramatic pause to heighten the Reds' enjoyment of the spectacle. But Jessica told Remmy of Hatch's true motivation. It had little to do with entertainment or rules.

Years ago, while Tam was going through the first phase of the infection and still mad, he rushed a small squad of ERC soldiers. Somehow, Tam managed to tear apart the soldiers with nothing more than his bare hands and teeth, but not before a soldier detonated a flash grenade beside Tam's face. The resulting blast had nearly blinded Tam in his left eye and rendered it almost useless in the dusky hours bridging night and day.

Hatch delayed the arena battle under the pretense of giving Remmy a rest, but what she really wanted was Tam with no depth perception and only one good eye. Staying on the left was Remmy's only chance of survival. But blind eye or not, Tam was still deadly.

The head of Tam's axe sailed past Remmy's face, the shrill whistle of the blade filling his ears as it sliced through the air. Avoiding the attacks was not going to be enough. Eventually, Tam would get lucky or Remmy would get tired. Remmy was going to have to fight, but he couldn't allow himself to become enraged. He couldn't allow the virus in.

The next attack went wide. Remmy figured that Tam's bad eye must be struggling with the dying light and murky depths created in the between hours of day and night. If he had any chance of winning, this was it.

As Tam closed in for another attack, Remmy backpedaled towards one of the wrecked cars. Timing was everything. A moment's hesitation would mean a slow painful death. He placed his back against its rusted skeleton and waited for Tam's swing.

Remmy ducked and rolled away from the attack, smiling slightly as he heard the screech of metal against metal. Tam had succeeded only in getting his axe stuck.

"I don't need that thing," Tam snarled as he gnashed his rows of pointed teeth and left the axe buried in the roof of the car. "This way will be much more fun!" He lunged forward, his pointed teeth bared and ready to tear flesh, but Tam's movements were clumsy and telegraphed, the product of arrogance and an underestimation of his challenger. Remmy again dropped to the left, avoiding Tam, but not before bringing the flat head of the axe crashing against Tam's knee. A sickening *crunch* filled the arena, but Tam remained standing, balancing on his one good leg. The leg Remmy smashed dangled, hanging at an unnatural angle and completely useless from the knee down.

"This isn't over!" Tam screeched, his words an equal mix of agony and rage. His knee was broken, the leg useless, but Tam refused to give in.

"We're done! You can't fight anymore!" Remmy growled, his shoulders heaving. He could feel anger spreading through his body, its toxic tendrils twisting through his innards and soul. Remmy's vision began to narrow to a pinpoint that showed nothing besides Tam. Red radiated like a bloody aura on the edges of his vision.

CORA! Remmy screamed in his own head. *Remember Cora!* Thoughts of Cora flooded Remmy's mind, leaving no place for anger and rage to take root. He had to hold on for her, he needed to see her again. She was worth fighting for, but not in the way that Jessica and the Reds wanted him to fight. Remmy refused to allow anger to overwhelm him. He slowed his breathing – in through his nose, out through his mouth. Again and again. Steady and slow. Deep breaths, thoughts of the fields, blue skies and the warmth of the sun began to force the anger from Remmy's body. There was still too much to live for, too much to enjoy. The electric sensation that Remmy felt when his lips touched Cora's shot through his body – the memory and feeling, one in the same.

"I'm done," Remmy announced to the crowd, the axe hanging at his side.

"Finish it!" Hatch demanded from the side of the arena. "The rules must be followed!"

"He can't fight anymore," Remmy shouted back. "He can barely stand! The fight's over."

"It has to end!" Hatch snapped. "It will end! You had better decide how it does, right now!"

A low growl rumbled behind Remmy's back.

"Remmy! Look out!" Jessica screamed. Hatch spun, slapping Jessica and knocking her out of her chair.

"Be silent!" Hatch hissed, but Jessica's eyes were fixed on the center of the arena.

Remmy turned in time to see Tam launch himself forward off his one good leg. He still had enough strength in that one leg to propel himself across the distance between him and Remmy.

The axe moved of its own volition. There would never be a memory of making the decision to swing the weapon. It simply moved. Remmy's reflexes took over, swinging the flat, hammer-like edge towards Tam's face. Tam, with no weapon of his own, led the attack with his teeth.

Tam's teeth were vicious, strong and dangerous, capable of shredding flesh and crushing bones, but they were no match for hardened steel. White, fragmented bits, tinged in red burst from the sides of Tam's mouth. His eyes went wide with shock and pain. A spray of blood followed as Remmy's swing drove deeper into Tam's mouth. The back corners of Tam's lips tore in jagged lines, giving him a permanent, crooked smile that spoke of nothing humorous. Remmy pulled the axe free. Tam collapsed to the ground. A disgusting gurgling mew rattled in Tam's throat as he choked on his own blood and teeth. Tam's teeth would eventually grow back, but his lower jaw hung unhinged and at a sickening angle. The fight was over.

"Well done!" Hatch applauded. "Now do what is right and kill him. The rules demand it!"

"No," Remmy said firmly. The bloodied axe fell to the ground. "I did what I had to survive, but I won't kill Tam. I won't become one of you. I don't care about your stupid, made up rules!"

"Do you hear that? The food doesn't want to fight anymore. It doesn't want to follow the rules," Hatch grinned. She had already gotten what she wanted. Tam was done, as good as dead and no longer a threat to her position. If Remmy no longer wanted to play nicely, well then, he could most assuredly serve another purpose.

The other Reds rose from their positions on the edges of the arena.

"If the food doesn't want to follow the rules," Hatch continued, "then you don't have to either, my friends. Dinner will have two courses tonight! Eat and be full!"

Hatch's words sent a jolt of electricity through the arena. The other Reds were on their feet, teeth bared and mouths open. Remmy watched as they dropped over the sides of the rusted school buses. He had beaten Tam, but was going to die anyway.

"Shuupid," Tam gurgled from the ground. He turned his head and vomited blood and teeth into the dirt. "Shuupid youman." A sickening laugh gurgled deep within Tam's throat, small red bubbles foaming from his broken mouth.

Hatch smiled, the situation was playing out better than she had expected. Not only was Tam out of the way, she also was feeding her people. As soon as the other Reds arrived, word of Hatch's actions would spread like wild fire and her position would be secure. The Reds would be united under her leadership and rule.

The satisfaction that Hatch felt left her blind to the fact that Jessica slowly crept up behind her. Hatch had been good to Jessica, had kept her safe from Tam, but Tam was gone now. It was a shame about Remmy though, he would have made a good Red, but some things just couldn't be helped.

What could be helped was Jessica's position and status. Hatch barely had time to utter a syllable of surprise before Jessica's jaws closed around the sides of her neck. With one strong pull, Jessica tore free a large, wet chunk of Hatch's neck. Hatch's words burbled and frothed in foamy red bubbles as Jessica chewed slowly, a toothy smile of deep satisfaction stretched across her young blood-spattered face.

Hatch stumbled across the roof of the bus. Jessica lunged forward and pulled Hatch's sword free from its scabbard. With one swift swing, Jessica freed Hatch's head from her body.

Blood streamed over the sides of the bus. Hatch's body lay tangled at Jessica's feet, bleeding and motionless. Jessica glared at the other Reds.

"Stop!" she screamed. "Stop right now!"

The Reds hesitated, stumbled a few steps forward. They were prepared for a feeding frenzy, ready to shred this human boy and the weakling, Tam. Those were the rules, but something in Jessica's voice made them stop. Slowly, all eyes turned towards the girl, her neck and face slick with the blood of their former leader.

"Hatch is dead!" Jessica boomed. "I've killed her. You'll all listen to me or die." Jessica pointed towards the Reds with the sword, Hatch's blood still dripping from the blade.

Some of the Reds mumbled dissent, but the look in Jessica's eyes silenced them. She looked feral and dangerous, even more so than the other Reds, even more so than Hatch. She had claimed her spot. Those were the rules. That was her right.

"Remmy lives," Jessica paused, "for now."

Remmy felt hands, filthy and calloused, close around his neck and arms. The Reds began dragging Remmy out of the arena, no doubt to put him back in that dingy rundown shack that had become his prison. The urge to fight swelled in Remmy's chest, but he fought it down and that was what the Reds wanted, what Jessica wanted.

As Remmy was pushed out of the arena, he wondered what lay ahead for him. Was this where his life would end or was he destined to keep fighting until he eventually gave in and became a Red or died? Both options seemed horrible. All Remmy wanted was to return to the peace of his fields, his waterfall…his Cora. Remmy's heart ached for Cora. Was their first kiss really destined to be their last? That seemed so unfair, so cruel. Why had fate bothered letting Remmy know what it was like to care about Cora and to have her care about him if he was never really going to be able to keep her?

A deep sigh escaped from Remmy's lips. He tilted his head up towards the darkening sky to watch the misty plume of his breath rise up into the air. At least some part of him was free to escape.

The sky seemed endless, so dark and expansive like an entire sea made of ink. Sadness pressed down upon Remmy. He imagined the endless darkness of the sky seeping into him, smudging his soul.

Looking up to release another breath, Remmy's eyes settled on a brilliant red star. How had he never noticed it before? Especially when it shone brighter than any other star or planet. The star appeared to expand, filling more of the sky and growing larger and larger.

The ground trembled ever so slightly under Remmy's feet as he was pushed back into the shed.

"What's going on?" Remmy demanded. None of the Reds answered, they were too busy staring at the sky, which was oddly enough becoming lighter instead of darker.

A blinding ruby red flash cut through the night sky. A pillar of light, no wider than a dinner plate, appeared in the center of the arena. The luminous column rapidly expanded, filling more and more of the arena. A few Reds slowly crept towards the light, unsure of what they were seeing. Most began to run.

Remmy stared for what could have only been seconds, but felt like hours, before he was thrown backwards into the shack by the blast that incinerated the arena. The buses forming the ring of the arena wilted under the intense heat of the flash, crumbling into twisted remains that no longer resembled what they once were. Outlines of Reds spiraled through the air. The bodies careened through the empty space surrounding the arena before crashing to the ground like meteors of charred meat and bone.

Outside the shack, Remmy heard the pounding of terrified footsteps and shouts. Large red spots swam through his vision, making it almost impossible to see. All the sounds were muffled, as if Remmy's head was packed in cotton, but somewhere in the insanity that swirled around him, Remmy was sure that he could hear someone calling his name.

-45-

The failed rescue had been embarrassing to say the least. An entire broadcast based upon fear and hatred for an enemy that wasn't there culminating with a dozen cows staring stupidly into the camera. Citizens expected death and victory. What had been delivered to them was a field full of cows.

Eldritch would have been furious if his Em-Pak allowed it, but he nonetheless found himself dissatisfied with the situation. Sure, Ortiz had swept two Emo camps before returning to the city and those successful campaigns were broadcast, but Eldritch could feel the questions of doubt quietly eroding the foundation of his power. It was simple logic. When a leader appears weak, contenders for the throne will emerge.

Eldritch's fingers tentatively touched the keyboard. He could easily ensure that no one ever questioned him again, could ensure that no citizen ever did anything that he would find unacceptable, but there were certain drawbacks to increasing everyone's Em-Pak signal, drawbacks that made Eldritch hesitate and decide not to.

An entire population of citizens like Ortiz and his men would be easy to control, but Eldritch imagined all of them standing in the middle of the roads or blankly staring at the walls of cubicles. They would be no better than the cows. The signal increase would create a loyal population, but one that would need to be babysat and directed at almost every turn. But even this was not why Eldritch paused.

What really kept him from punching the keys required to subjugate all citizens was the challenge, the thrill of victory. With no emotions, all that remained to give Eldritch any sense of accomplishment was intelligence and victory. He would outsmart the citizens and maintain his control without the use of increased Em-Pak signals, because that would make his success that much sweeter.

Still, thoughts of all those doughy-eyed cows haunted Eldritch. Was there some remnant of concern for his family, some long since forgotten shard of love that festered and nagged at the back of his mind?

No, Eldritch thought, that wasn't why he perseverated upon the failed rescue mission. His family was a political prop and could continue to be so, alive or dead. What plagued him like a cut on the roof of his mouth that he couldn't stop opening and reopening with his tongue, was the fact that someone had outsmarted him. Who would have the know-how and intelligence required to reroute an ERC emergency signal? That required an understanding of the technology and access to it that was well beyond anything they had ever seen from an Emo and certainly not a Red. Then who? Who understood the working of ERC satellites and radio transmissions?

Eldritch shuddered as if the temperature had suddenly dropped in his office. *Was it possible? But how? There was no way!* All these thoughts ricocheted through Eldritch's mind as another shudder passed through his body. He couldn't shake the feeling that a ghost stood behind him, its cold hands slowly wrapping around his neck.

"How could he?" Eldritch wondered. "He's dead. There's no way." But Eldritch was a logical man and when all other options were eliminated, what remained, no matter how unlikely, was the answer.

Eldritch's fingers began to fly across his keyboard. They had been able to trace the ERC SOS signal back to the satellite that transmitted it, albeit falsely, into that field of cows. From there, the signal was lost in a mishmash of encryption and rerouting through countless other sources. But one thing still remained that presented Eldritch with a splinter of hope. The transmission had been sent from a source on the ground and that source could possibly be triangulated. A ground-based signal would most likely be small, lacking any major broadcasting power, so it would need to employ the nearest tower and satellite to send its signal successfully.

Punching a few more keys, Eldritch cued a screen showing the paths of multiple ERC satellites. He wound the timeframe back to the day the emergency signal began transmitting. The area that the signal had come from only had two available satellites nearby. A few more keystrokes brought up the activity logs for both satellites. Nothing appeared out of the ordinary.

"Damn it," 'Eldritch growled. "Where are you?" His eyes narrowed as he studied the numbers and activities. Nothing but ERC approved transmissions. Could the signal be hidden in one of these? That was likely, but that also meant that Eldritch could spend a lifetime sorting through the hundreds of thousands of transmissions that were sent in a single day and still be no closer to finding the source. There was only one person Eldritch would credit with being this devious, this intelligent – his father.

A loud *ping* from the computer caused Eldritch to look up from where he had buried his head in his hands. The satellite activity log showed something strange. A third satellite had deviated from its orbit and was entering the space of the two satellites Eldritch was currently studying. However, this one was very different from the other two. Those two were little more than communications satellites, capable of tracking and sending communications, useful for spying and taking intel pictures. That was not the use of the third satellite, a satellite that had been kept private, even from some of the most high-ranking politicians. But Eldritch knew this satellite well, remembered his father showing him the plans for it and excitedly describing how it would bring an end to all wars. The movement of this satellite left no doubt in Eldritch's mind. His father was alive.

The ERC military satellite moved into position over a large clearing and began powering up. The gas particles contained within the glass cylinders would be agitated, forced to bounce off one another faster and faster, releasing energy with each collision. This energy would soon reach critical mass resulting in the release of a massive beam of light and a searing explosion. Eldritch could have tried to override the satellite. There was undoubtedly a failsafe programmed into it, but curiosity prevented him. Why was this person, who most likely was his long dead father, powering up one of the most deadly weapons in the ERC's arsenal and discharging it into the middle of nowhere?

As if in answer to Eldritch's question, his phone beeped loudly and began to vibrate. The emergency signal was once again transmitting and this time the coordinates were almost identical to those of the military satellite. Eldritch opened his phone, silenced the SOS transmission and called Ortiz.

"Captain!" Eldritch snapped. "Get your men to this location immediately. I am sending you the coordinates now."

"Yes, sir," Ortiz answered. "Coordinates were received. One thing though, Mr. Eldritch, sir?"

"What? What is it?" Eldritch demanded. "Time is off the essence, Ortiz!"

"Of course," Ortiz responded, "but Mr. Eldritch, these coordinates are almost in the exact location of reports we just received regarding a massive explosion. Could they be connected?"

"Damn it, Ortiz!" Eldritch shouted. "Congratulations! You are a freaking genius! Of course, they must be connected. Now get in your little car and go figure out what the hell is happening!"

"Yes, sir," Ortiz said. "Immediately, sir."

"One more thing, Ortiz," Eldritch said slowly, "and this is strictly between the two of us."

"Yes sir," Ortiz agreed.

Eldritch took a deep breath and exhaled. The beeping of his Em-Pak could be heard in the background. "If by chance you see any of my family members, I want them brought back alive."

"Of course, Mr. Eldritch," Ortiz answered, as if there was really no reason for clarification. Why wouldn't Assemblyman Eldritch want his family brought back alive? Wasn't that why Ortiz was still chipping cow crap off his boots?

"Ortiz!" Eldritch shouted. "I mean *any - ANY* of my family members! Even dead ones!"

"Dead ones?" Ortiz asked, his own Em-Pak beeping now. Was Assemblyman Eldritch beginning to crack under the weight of his new position? He wouldn't have been the first politician to lose it because of the pressure. "Sir, how can I bring back the dead ones alive? I'm sorry, Mr. Eldritch, but I'm not understanding these orders."

"Listen to me *very* carefully, Ortiz," Eldritch seethed. "I have reason to believe that my father may be involved in this current situation. To what degree and in what manner I know not, but if he is there, I want him brought in alive and away from the cameras. Everything and everyone else is fair game, Captain. We need this to look good, Ortiz, not like last time. Because God help me, Ortiz, if I so much as see a cow this time, they're not going to be the only ones that need to worry about being ground up."

"Understood, sir," Ortiz answered, as he looked down at his boots, still caked and filthy and then added, "Perfectly, Mr. Eldritch, sir."

-46-

A red spot formed miles above the circle of buses, barely noticeable among the smattering of stars in the night sky. Cora was terrified to see that Samuel and Xander had been right - the Reds were forcing Remmy to fight in some sort of sick arena. But she remained with Samuel on a wooded rise and waited.

It was hard for Cora to keep quite as a large Red chased after Remmy swinging an axe and gnashing his wicked looking teeth. Remmy was doing a good job avoiding the attacks, but had yet to fight back. He was going to need to do something to buy some time. He needed to last until Samuel's red dot did whatever it was supposed to do.

"Not much of a fighter," Xander shrugged as he watched the arena through a pair of binoculars. "Lover boy is going to need to find some nerve if he's going to last much longer."

"Shut up, Xander!" Cora spat through her teeth.

The large Red swung his axe, getting it stuck in the rusted roof of an old junker. The Red dropped the axe and lunged forward, but this time Remmy dropped low, smashing his axe into the Red's knee. Cora smiled as the Red's scream filled the arena. Remmy turned to yell something at the other Reds. Cora couldn't hear, but she could see the other Reds getting anxious.

"Uh oh," Xander mumbled as he watched the Red launch himself towards Remmy on his one good leg. "It's not over yet. Lover boy should have finished the job when that Red was out of commission."

"What?" Cora cried. She watched as Remmy swung the axe once more, this time aiming for the Red's face. The spray of blood and teeth was visible even from where Cora sat. Remmy's face was red and twisted with rage and Cora momentarily worried that she had lost him – that everything had been for nothing. Remmy's face relaxed, returning to its regular color. He was back, had never been gone. There was still time.

"Samuel," Cora pleaded, "how much longer do we have to wait? Remmy won't last much longer." Her grandfather lay on his back staring up at the night sky, as if watching the stars were his only care in the world.

"Right there," Samuel pointed at the red spot. "As soon as Remmy is clear, I'll do my part. Watch that until it gets a bit bigger, but then avert your eyes. You're going to need to be able to see to save Remmy."

"Oh boy, Cora," Xander called still watching the arena, "you're going to want to see this."

Cora rolled away from Samuel and pressed the binoculars to her eyes. The Reds were dropping over the sides of the buses and heading towards Remmy. Countless pairs of hands closed around Remmy and pulled him out of the arena.

"But he won!" Cora protested.

"I don't think they care," Xander answered.

"Cora. Xander," Samuel called. "You might want to cover your eyes." They turned to see Samuel prone on the ground, his eyes shielded behind his folded arms.

The sky lightened, as if the sun were rising early. Cora covered her eyes and hoped that Remmy could survive whatever was about to happen.

A concussive *BOOM* split the night. Wave after wave of intense heat rolled through the clearing surrounding the Red camp. Cora felt her back getting hot, imagining that her clothes and hair might catch fire. How could Remmy survive this?

"Let's go!" Samuel shouted. "Remember how to use your wrist guns?"

"Aim and flick?" Xander mocked as he looked at the device. He would never admit that they slightly impressed him.

"Come on," Cora called. She was already over the rise and heading towards the Red camp.

"It looks like they took Remmy to that building," Samuel shouted as he checked his wrist screen and pointed at a run-down shack.

Cora immediately corrected her path and headed towards the building. A Red rushed towards her from the left side. The Red's eyes were wild and shot with blood. Half of her hair had had been singed off by Samuel's attack and still smoldered on the side of her head. The blade raised over her head, though slightly blackened by the fire, still posed a very real threat. Cora froze, the insanity of the Red rooting her feet to the ground.

Xander didn't hesitate. A loud *poof* burst beside Cora's head. Seconds later, countless tiny red wounds blossomed on the Red's face. Both the blade and Red fell to the ground.

"Um...thank you," Cora said, the words almost sounding like a question.

Xander laughed dryly as he reloaded his wrist gun. "Save your sisterly gushing," Xander grinned sarcastically. "I just saw a chance to kill a Red and wanted to do it before you could. That's one for me, zero for you."

Cora wanted to believe that some part of Xander had wanted to protect her, wanted to keep her safe because she was his sister. Emotions swirled in Cora's heart, a mix of both ends of the spectrum, creating a feeling of unease that she did her best to push down. The polarized feelings she felt towards her brother could be dealt with after Remmy was safe. The ramshackle little shed was right up ahead. Remmy was so close to safety, so close to Cora.

"Three to zero!" Xander shouted as he took down another Red. He had found an axe somewhere and was now using it more than his wrist gun. He appeared to enjoy a more hands on approach. "Four!" Xander grunted bringing the axe down with a sickening *thud, squish.*

Three Reds rushed Cora from the sides of the shed.

"I've got the two on the left!" Samuel shouted and rushed forward. Cora saw her grandfather fire a shot that dropped one Red, but the second still came forward, tackling Samuel.

"Samuel!" Cora yelled. The third Red was within arm's reach of her. Cora leapt backwards and tilted her hand upward, releasing the compressed air and tightly packed steel buckshot. The Red's head was almost sheared in half from being shot at such close range. Cora was splattered with a slick of the Red's blood and bits of gore. She wanted to puke, but Samuel, her grandfather, needed her.

"Five to one!" Xander yelled as he rushed past Cora towards Samuel. "You're not stealing this one!"

"Damn it, Xander, no one is keeping track! Help Samuel!" Cora shouted and raced after her brother. He had been distracted by an easier target and left Samuel to the mercy of the Red. All questions regarding Xander's motivation were answered. With no emotions to color his actions, this was little more than a game to Xander.

"Six to one! You'd better step it up, Cora!" Xander taunted as he wrenched his axe free from the shoulder of a now dead Red.

Samuel wrestled with the Red, showing the strength of a man twenty years younger, but the Red was still stronger.

"Go, Cora!" Samuel said as he fought the Red. "Get Remmy while there's still confusion!"

Cora hesitated.

"GO!" Samuel demanded. The Red's teeth snapped closed just inches from his face.

"Seven!" Xander bellowed and pressed the barrel of his wrist gun against the side of the Red's head. The Red's eyes showed a moment of confusion, a touch of fear having felt the cold metal of the gun.

The Red's head disappeared in a large cloud of red. Ragged, wet bits rained down around Xander and Samuel. Cora pushed the disturbing image out of her mind and ran towards Remmy. She could see him through the open door of the shed. He was on the ground, but moving. Cora hoped that he was only stunned.

"Remmy!" Cora shouted. "Remmy get up. Get up!" Cora could hear feet pounding the ground behind her, but something hummed beneath the noise. Was Samuel firing up the satellite again? Couldn't be. Cora remembered her grandfather saying that they would only get one shot, but what was the noise? It sounded like an entire army of enraged bees. A *thrum-thrum-thrum* muted all the sounds around Cora, filled her ears and made her bones feel like they were vibrating.

"Samuel?" Cora called over her shoulder. Her grandfather, covered with gore, shook his head.

"It's not me, Cora," Samuel shouted over the sound, "but I really, really think we need to get moving now."

Three black ERC helicopters emerged from behind the trees. A small army of heavy military vehicles kept pace below the helicopters. Cora's eyes widened as she the heavy multi-barreled machine guns begin to spin.

"Remmy! Remmy!" Cora screamed. She dashed into the shack and yanked him from the ground. "Remmy, we need to go now!"

"Cora?" Remmy asked weakly as he rubbed his eyes and struggled to stand. "Cora, what are you doing here?"

Cora opened her mouth to answer, but her words were lost beneath the high-pitched whine of the helicopter's machine guns. Clouds of dirt leapt up from the ground around them as Cora and Remmy ran from the shack. A moment's hesitation and they would have been chewed to bits and lost in the splintered remains of the building.

-47-

Captain Ortiz wished that his Em-Pak would stop beeping. The other ERC soldiers in his truck glanced around trying to determine whose Em-Pak was responsible for all the noise. The truth was that they were all guilty. All of the men could see what lay before them and if they had any sense and no Em-Pak, would have been terrified. Sadly, the ERC soldiers, Ortiz included, had neither of these luxuries and blindly followed Assemblyman Eldritch's orders to track the signal to its source.

A wave of Reds, at least twenty across and four deep raced towards Ortiz and his men. They had at first appeared confused, maybe even a little scared, but now they just looked angry. Weapons, crude but vicious, were raised high overhead. The helicopters strafed the lines of Reds with machine gun fire, but for every one Red that fell, two appeared to take its place.

Ortiz, even with his modified Em-Pak, could do the simple math of the battle. More bodies than bullets would always win. If there were enough Reds, they would eventually overrun Ortiz and his men.

"Mr. Eldritch, sir?" Ortiz called into his radio. "We have a situation here, sir."

"I can see that, Captain," Eldritch growled, "but what I don't see is you dealing with it. Are you calling to resign your position? Because if you're not, then may I strongly suggest that you start doing your damn job and track down the source of that signal!"

"Understood, sir," Ortiz answered and clicked off his radio. "Lock and load men. We're going to engage the enemy."

"Sir! Yes sir!" the ERC soldiers answered in unison. Once Ortiz and his men were out of their vehicles, the helicopters would have to stop firing and provide intel. Ortiz couldn't risk losing any men to friendly fire. He was going to need every single soldier if they were going to survive this and complete the mission.

The helicopters pulled back, splitting off from one another and circling the clearing.

"Go now, Captain!" one of the helicopter pilots called through the radio. "There's a break in the enemy lines!"

"You heard them!" Ortiz shouted and leapt from the driver's seat. He checked the magazine on his machine gun, flicked the safety and prepared to face countless Reds.

The helicopter pilot had been correct, there was a break in the Reds' lines, but only a brief one that quickly closed around Ortiz and his men. Shots went wild as the Reds surged forward, dragging soldiers to the ground, tearing into them with weapons and teeth alike.

"Stay focused on the mission!" Ortiz shouted. "Clear a path! We need to find the source of that signal!" The ERC soldiers silently nodded their agreement and focused their firing on a single column of Reds. Bodies crumpled under the hail of bullets, opening a space for Ortiz and his men.

"We've got space, Captain!" a soldier yelled. He turned to face Ortiz and left himself blind to the Red that leapt from behind him, dragging him to the ground and savagely tearing into his throat with row upon row of pointed teeth.

Ortiz paused to shoot the Red in the face before leading the charge through the opening his troops had made. Reds came from all sides, surging like storm waves battering the helpless edges of the shoreline, but each surge of Reds were pushed back by round after round of machine gun fire. Ortiz could see that each attack cost him at least one soldier, if not more. He would need to move and keep moving. The math was rapidly getting worse and Ortiz could sense the odds drastically tipping away from his favor.

"Report, Captain!" Eldritch's voice barked through the radio in Ortiz's helmet.

"Tracking...damn it!" Ortiz cried as a Red clamped down on his arm. He pulled his pistol from its leg holster and shot the Red in the temple. It fell to the ground, but not before leaving a bloody ring of holes gaping on Ortiz's arm. "Sorry, sir," Ortiz continued. "We're tracking the signal now." Ortiz paused to fire a few rounds. "We're close. Within fifty feet of the source, Mr. Eldritch, sir. Still no sign of your family members, sir." A few more rounds chewed into the side of another Red who wildly swung a gnarled club.

"Carry on, Captain," Eldritch's voice commanded, "find that source!"

"Understood, sir," Ortiz gasped as he flexed his injured arm to bring up his machine gun. Blood streaked down Ortiz's arm, soaking into his uniform and sticking the material to his side.

The Reds finally began to fall back, their attacks becoming intermittent. Ortiz was thankful for the break, but something about the Reds' behavior worried him. They were acting as if they had a plan, some idea as to what they were doing. Ortiz, like all citizens, had been taught by the ERC that the Reds were mindless animals, capable of little more than violence and the basest instincts. The Reds pulled back, regrouping near the smoldering remains of a circle of vehicles.

"Signal, Lieutenant?" Ortiz grunted as he picked off a few of the retreating Reds.

"It's coming from somewhere near that building, Captain," the soldier responded, "or at least what's left of it."

Ortiz nodded and began moving towards the remains of what looked like it had once been a shed of some sort. A boy ran from the ruins with a girl close behind. No, not just any girl, it was Cora Eldritch and a ghost followed close behind. Another boy hesitated near the wreckage, as if unsure of what to do. He eventually turned and followed behind the others. It was Xander Eldritch.

"Mr. Eldritch," Ortiz panted as he chased after Cora. "We've located the source of the signal. I've got eyes on your children, and well, I'm not sure how to say this, but what appears to be your father as well, sir. There's also an unidentified boy, sir."

"My father," Eldritch responded, his words more of a statement than a question. "Follow your orders, Captain. Collect my family members, alive. Everyone else is expendable."

"Understood, sir," Ortiz snapped and then turned to his soldiers. "You know the orders. Collect the members of the Eldritch family. Anyone else is expendable." As Ortiz finished his words, a soldier cried out in pain.

The Em-Pak could prevent or erase numerous feelings, but pain was not one of them. The soldier bore a ragged wound on his right side. He desperately tried to stuff his spilled innards back into the gaping hole, but to no avail.

"Captain?" the soldier asked before his eyes rolled back and he tumbled to the ground with a sickeningly wet slap.

A small Red, no more than ten or so, crouched behind the now dead soldier. The Red chewed slowly, her pointed teeth jutting out at odd angles from her mouth. Ortiz momentarily thought that at one point this girl probably would have been a prime candidate for braces and then shook the idea from his head. He fired.

More Reds were approaching. A young girl, or at least what had once been a young girl, appeared to be giving orders. The Reds split into two groups, the larger of the two closing in on Ortiz and his men. The smaller group of Reds, including their apparent leader, broke off and trailed after the Eldritch family.

"Engage the Reds!" Ortiz ordered. "Keep our exit clear! I'm going after the Eldritch family."

"Alone, Captain?" one of the ERC soldiers asked, not out of concern, rather just as a point of clarification.

"We need a clear exit. That means every able gun is pointed at the Reds," Ortiz barked. "I'll get the targets and then we're gone."

Ortiz turned and sprinted after his targets. His lungs burned from the heavy clouds of cordite that hung in the air. The smell coated Ortiz's mouth, drying the inside and filling it with a taste similar to blood. Ortiz's Em-Pak chirped loudly, but the sound was lost beneath that of countless machine gun rounds and the screams of ERC soldiers.

Remmy's ears still rang, but the red spots no longer swam through his vision. Cora pulled him from the floor and yanked him out of the shed seconds before it disappeared in a hail of bullets and splinters. The scene that awaited Remmy felt surreal, almost impossible. Countless Reds attacked ERC soldiers while three black helicopters darted back and forth like angry wasps.

"Remmy, we need to go!" Cora shouted as she shook his shoulder. She grabbed his wrist and pulled. Remmy, his head clearing, suddenly seemed to comprehend Cora's words and began running. Her hand began to slip from Remmy's wrist, but he twisted his hand and grabbed Cora's, their fingers intertwined.

"I'm not losing you twice," Remmy grinned, his words sounded rough, his throat choked with dust, but the look on his face spoke of nothing but love.

Samuel and Xander were outside, both looking like they had passed through Hell to get here. Only Xander appeared unfazed by the killing and chaos. Remmy chalked it up to the influence of the boy's Em-Pak, though he couldn't truly be sure.

"This way!" Samuel pointed to a narrow path that disappeared into the woods. Remmy and Cora ran to keep up, but Xander hesitated near the ruins of the shed.

"Xander!" Samuel cried. "Xander, we must leave now! Please, come with us!"

Xander remained still. A massive pack of Reds streamed towards the ERC soldiers he stared at. Xander appeared to be weighing his options. With no apparent way to reach the ERC soldiers, Xander turned and ran towards the woods.

"How did you find me?" Remmy panted as he willed his legs to move faster. His fingers remained locked with Cora's.

"Samuel," Cora gasped. "He found you, but can't we discuss this later?"

"Good idea," Remmy agreed.

"Cora!" Xander screeched, his voice momentarily panicked and laced with pain.

Remmy, Samuel and Cora skidded a few steps before turning to see Xander pinned to the ground by a young Red. The girl's face was badly burned on one side, her white teeth appearing to glow against the blackened skin.

"Leaving so soon?" Jessica grinned as she loomed over Xander.

"Jessica stop! Please!" Remmy shouted. He turned to run back, but Cora's grip on his hand remained steadfast, her fingers strong and unyielding as steel bars.

"Jessica?" Cora asked. "Remmy? What is going on?"

"I knew her," Remmy answered. "I know her." Cora's grip weakened ever so slightly. "I'll be okay, Cora, I promise. You need to let me help Xander."

"You know her?" Cora asked, feeling jealousy for the first time. "How could you know her?"

"Cora, please," Remmy pulled away. "Later, right?"

Cora hesitated. She wanted Remmy back, needed him back. Xander was her brother and Cora didn't want anything to happen to him, but Xander refused to change. Would Cora really risk having Remmy back for Xander? Remmy brought joy and love into Cora's life. He made her feel complete. Xander was the antithesis of all of these feelings, but he was still her brother.

"Jessica, let him go," Remmy demanded. Cora let go of his hand, a decision that felt harder than any she had ever made before. Remmy turned, locking his eyes with Cora's, and smiled. It was a small smile, little more than a curl of the corner of Remmy's lips, but it made Cora's heart tighten and flutter.

"Be careful," Cora whispered as she watched Remmy slowly approach the snarling Red named Jessica.

"You could have had it all, Remmy!" Jessica cried. "You could have been a king! My king! Look at what I did for you! I killed Hatch to keep you safe and you try to run away? What kind of thanks is that for all that I have done? For keeping you safe for so long?"

"Jessica," Remmy said softly, "I'm not like you. I'm not a Red. I don't want this. I don't want to be a king."

"What!" Jessica shouted. Xander squirmed beneath her. Jessica opened her jaws revealing rows of wicked teeth. She dragged a few dagger-like points across Xander's cheek, carving ruby red lines into the soft flesh. "Be still food," Jessica threatened. "Keep fighting and I might just get hungry." She licked Xander's blood from her teeth. A predatory smile, like a cat toying with a bird, stretched across Jessica's face as she returned her gaze to Remmy. Xander stopped moving, his eyes fixed on the Red's teeth.

"I appreciate what you did for me, Jessica," Remmy began. He slowly moved towards her and Xander. "I really do, but you can't force that life on me."

"How do you *force* freedom on someone, Remmy?" Jessica sneered. "That's just stupid. I offered you the freedom to live without fear. But you'd rather scamper off with *her*? And what, Remmy? What will your life be like? I'll tell you what! You'll live every day in fear of infection, fear of the Reds and fear of the ERC! How is that living?"

"I don't know, Jessica," Remmy answered, "but that's my life. It was yours too. Remember the camp? Remember my parents? Remember your parents, Jessica?"

A look of true sadness crept into Jessica's eyes. The insanity seemed to waver like the dying flame of a candle. She looked as if she were trying to force back her emotions and bury the memories. Jessica snapped her teeth one more time, but all threat was gone. She stood, looming over Xander, her teeth bared.

"Get up, food," Jessica growled. "You're lucky Remmy was here. Lucky that I still have some memory of who I was. Lucky that I'm not hungry." Jessica paused and turned her gaze to Remmy. She appeared sad. "I do remember, Remmy. That's why I was trying to keep you here. I remember everyone, especially you. I miss them all the time. I'm lonely all the time, Remmy. It's awful. I just wanted some of those feelings to go away, even just a little bit."

"Jessica," Remmy began. He had no idea what he was going to say. Could he really tell her to come with them? What was he expecting?

"Leave, Remmy," Jessica snarled, a claw-like finger pointing towards the woods. "Leave now before I change my mind."

"Thank you," Remmy nodded. Jessica's shoulders trembled slightly. Remmy couldn't tell if it was from rage or tears. Maybe it was both.

A shadow moved behind Jessica and Xander, something large and menacing. Thoughts of Tam flooded Remmy's mind, but Tam was dead.

"*JESSICA!*" Remmy screamed as the soldier leveled his gun with the back of her head. Remmy dove forward, not knowing what he planned to do, but determined to save someone who had once been a friend, no matter what she had become.

-49-

Eldritch watched with as much pride and satisfaction as his Em-Pak would allow. The battle raged on his video monitor and in every home, in every city controlled by the ERC. The citizens would now see first-hand and up close, what they were up against. Sure, the fake Emo attacks had shaken some citizens up, but this was something different. This was real.

Now citizens would see what waited for their children if they refused to follow along with Eldritch. Now they understood the gravity of the situation. Their children were hostages of the ERC, of Eldritch, and he alone would decide who lived and who died.

"Mr. Eldritch?" Ortiz's voice whispered through the radio. The Captain was silently creeping towards a Red that loomed over Xander. This would make for amazing footage. Hopefully, the camera on Captain Ortiz's helmet would capture it.

"Go ahead, Captain," Eldritch grinned. His Em-Pak beeped and the smile faded.

"Sir, the Red has Xander pinned," Ortiz reported.

"I can see that, Ortiz," Eldritch snapped, returning to his characteristic unpleasant demeanor. "What is it?"

"Should I fire, sir?" Ortiz questioned. "Your children...and your father are within the kill zone." Ortiz still found it hard to believe that he was reporting the fact that Samuel Eldritch Sr. was alive and well.

"Oh, just kill that nasty creature and get on with it," Eldritch demanded. "As long as I have one child left and my father is brought back alive, I will consider this operation a success. Cora would be ideal, Xander is...well, Xander is acceptable." Eldritch said the word as if it tasted foul. He had invested so much time and effort into Cora's future. She was simply the more logical choice. But if he had to start over with Xander then so be it.

"Understood, sir," Ortiz answered and moved forward. The Red was busy, unaware of the proximity of Ortiz and the promise of death carried in his hands.

The Red gnashed its teeth near Xander's face and Xander froze.

"Smart boy," Ortiz whispered. "Fighting that thing won't end well. Just stay still a little bit longer." Ortiz raised his gun, preparing to fire, but the Red suddenly stood up. It looked down at Xander and spoke, and released the boy to whoever the other boy was.

Ortiz lined up the shot and prepared to end this, to achieve his objective and get the hell out of here before the Reds did anything else strange.

"*JESSICA!*" the unknown boy screeched and dove towards the Red.

"Jessica?" Ortiz mumbled, his face pressed against the stock of his gun. Who would name a Red Jessica? Who would bother naming a Red anything? No matter.

Ortiz's moment of hesitation gave the boy time to reach the Red. Ortiz squeezed the trigger, but the boy's momentum carried the Red out of the line of fire. The shot caught her on the corner of her shoulder, a painful injury, but far from fatal. Ortiz prepared his next shot, lined it up perfectly on the Red evenly between the V of his sight. *Click...click...click.* Ortiz had lost count of his shots in the insanity of the battle. He dropped his machine gun and began fumbling with the clasp that held his sidearm in its holster.

The Red pushed the boy off her and turned to face Ortiz. She looked at her shoulder. The injury did nothing beyond anger her.

The Reds were animals, Ortiz had been taught that. But these Reds had shown something very different. They had shown intelligence. At this moment though, those thoughts mattered little.

The Red snarled, small pillows of foam in the corners of her mouth. Her eyes narrowed, the pupils constricted to small coal pinpoints that bore into Ortiz. She clashed her pointed teeth together and glared at Ortiz. Right now, this Red was very much a wild animal, an injured one at that, which meant she was far more dangerous.

Ortiz's Em-Pak began its frantic electronic tittering as the Red dropped low to the ground and launched herself towards him, her jaws stretching open to an unbelievable width. Ortiz's hands were slow and clumsy, fumbling with his sidearm. The weapon slipped from his grip and clattered to the ground, the noise resonating in Ortiz's head like the tone of his own funeral bells.

-50-

The Red was going to die, or at least should. Xander really couldn't have cared less. That thing was filthy, disgusting and it had put its grimy hands on him. It had threatened him, cut him with her teeth and called him *food* of all things! Xander wanted that Red dead on the ground, riddled with bullets and slowly bleeding to death. He wanted all the Reds dead and the Emos too for that matter.

What Xander did care about was the soldier that currently fumbled with his sidearm, trying to stop the Red from peeling his skin like a banana. That soldier looked familiar. He looked like someone he had seen with his father, but that didn't matter. All that mattered was that this man was an ERC soldier and surely would take Xander back to his father, and back to the life he was born to live.

"Xander, let's go," Cora's dirty little Emo pet shouted, pulling at his clothes.

"Get off of me!" Xander snapped.

"Xander please," Samuel pleaded. "We need to leave."

"I am leaving," Xander responded, "leaving all of this garbage and insanity. I'm returning to father." Xander snapped an arm around Remmy's neck, pulling it into a tight hold. "Listen very carefully, Remmy. Don't do anything stupid. You even think about something I don't like and that's it." Xander pressed the barrel of his wrist gun into the side of Remmy's head. "One flick of my wrist and your head is gone. Got it?"

"Xander, what are you doing?" Cora cried and started forward. Samuel's hand shot out and grabbed his granddaughter.

"Cora, don't," Samuel warned. "Xander will kill him." It was clear that his grandson had made his decision.

"Samuel," Cora said weakly. She had come so close to saving Remmy and now her own brother was going to kill him.

"Hey! You, the disgusting Red!" Xander shouted. "Don't or Remmy dies!"

The Red stopped. She had knocked the soldier to the ground and was circling back to finish the job.

"Jessica," Remmy gritted, "her name is Jessica."

"Fine," Xander sneered. "*Jessica*, let that soldier up or I split Remmy's head in half."

Jessica snarled. Her teeth clashed together with such force that it sounded as if they had cracked. The pearly rows of gleaming bone daggers remained intact.

"Remmy," Jessica growled, her voice low and full of violence. "Remmy, this is getting to be old."

Xander could see more Reds heading towards them.

"Get up!" Xander snapped, glaring at the soldier. "What is your name?" The young boy's voice carried all the authority of his father's.

"Ortiz," the soldier answered, "Captain Ortiz. Your father sent me to rescue you."

"About damn time," Xander sneered and yanked Remmy towards the soldier.

"Xander please," Cora shouted. "Please stop this. Remmy saved you. Saved you twice! Just let him go! You don't have to stay, but let him go!" Cora could feel the hard, cold barrel of her own wrist gun pressed against her arm. She had one shot left. Would she really use it to kill Xander?

"Ms. Eldritch," Ortiz yelled, his gun held at half ready, "your father has sent me to take you home. To take all of you home, even you Mr. Eldritch."

"Young man," Samuel shook his head, "I'll be going nowhere with you and neither will my granddaughter. If Xander has chosen to leave, then that is his choice, but you must let Remmy go." Samuel did his best to play into the persona of the person the ERC had created in his image.

"Let him go?" Ortiz asked. "Mr. Eldritch, are you feeling well, sir? That boy is the only thing keeping the Reds at bay right now. The last thing I'll be doing is asking Xander to let him go."

Xander moved beside Captain Ortiz. He still kept his arm tightly wrapped around Remmy's throat, the barrel of his gun still pressed to the side of Remmy's head.

Jessica paced, her energy and anger becoming more frantic. Cora could see that she wasn't going to be able to control herself for much longer. She needed to get Remmy free immediately.

"Sir?" Ortiz called into the radio inside his helmet. "Are you seeing this, Mr. Eldritch?"

"Yes," Eldritch mumbled as he frantically punched keys on his computer. Thinking that his children were dead, he had never bothered to check the signal being transmitted from their Em-Paks. Had he actually cared about rescuing them, as opposed to using their deaths for political gain, he would have checked the signals long ago and found that Cora's reported a malfunction and then went silent. Xander's still transmitted loud and clear. "Captain Ortiz," Eldritch said slowly.

"Yes sir?" Ortiz answered, his word distracted and quick. He kept his sidearm trained on Jessica. The Red wasn't going to play ball for much longer. Xander had the Emo subdued. The boy showed some real promise.

"Ortiz, listen to me very, very carefully," Eldritch's voice came through the radio, his words tipped in venom. "Cora has deactivated her Em-Pak. She is an Emo terrorist, and so is my father. If you can subdue either of them do so, but otherwise they are to be given no special consideration. They are terrorists and I expect you to treat them as such." Eldritch paused and took a deep breath, exhaling slowly. "On second thought, just kill them, Ortiz. They made their decision and I will not suffer the embarrassment of it. Do you understand, Captain?"

"Understood, sir," Ortiz grinned. "Perfectly." This made the math of battle a little easier to calculate and balance. It removed a few problematic variables. Ortiz turned to face Cora and Samuel. His face no longer held the look of a rescuing hero. No, now Ortiz's face was set in the hardened mask of a seasoned soldier.

Cora felt as if the air chilled. Goosebumps covered her arms and legs. The small hairs on the back of her neck stood on end. Something about Ortiz's look was very bad.

"Let Remmy go and we're gone," Cora offered, but it appeared to have no effect on Ortiz or Xander.

"Ms. Eldritch," Ortiz said, his eyes narrowed and cold, "I'm going to ask you one time and only one time to lay down your weapon. Mr. Eldritch, I suggest you do the same. Your next decision will determine if I bring you back to the city in a helicopter or a body bag. What's it going to be?"

1

"He knows we've deactivated our Em-Paks," Samuel whispered to Cora. "Go along with what he says."

Cora and Samuel unstrapped their wrist guns and tossed them to the ground. They then stepped back slowly, hands raised in surrender.

"Very good," Ortiz nodded. He swung the barrel of his pistol level with Cora's face. Ortiz had no patience for terrorist, no matter what their last name was. These two were never going back to the city.

Remmy watched as Ortiz's finger flexed on the trigger. Time seemed to slow down, moving with the gummy stubbornness of honey. Cora was going to die. She was going to be gunned down and Remmy would be forced to watch.

"Remmy! Now!" Jessica snarled as she launched herself at Ortiz. Her jaws clamped around his extended arm. Bones splintered, crushed beneath the pressure of her powerful teeth and jaws. Ortiz cried out in pain. The gun fell from his hand, clattering to the ground. Half of his arm followed close behind.

Remmy, sensing that time was short, stamped down on Xander's left foot with all the force he could muster. Xander yelped in pain, the small bones of his foot crunched under Remmy's heavy boot. His grip loosened and Remmy wrenched Xander's arm from around his neck. Bending Xander's elbow in the wrong direction, Remmy used the motion to flip the boy over his shoulder. Xander's wrist gun went off with a loud poof, peppering the ground near Remmy's foot with metal shot.

Ortiz stumbled backwards, a look of pure shock etched into his face. He stared wide-eyed at his ruined arm that ended in a ragged, wet stump. Ortiz's mouth silently mouthed words of disbelief. How had he been so stupid? He never should have taken his eyes and even more importantly, his gun, off the Red. Ortiz thumped to the ground like an oversized toddler, his legs splayed out.

Jessica walked forward, her eyes burning with hunger and rage. "Usually," Jessica smiled a toothy grin at Ortiz, "I don't like my food aged. It makes the meat tough and stringy!" She lunged forward, gnashing her teeth together. "But this time, oh my, my, my. This time I'm going to make an exception." She dove towards

Ortiz, but Remmy wrapped his arms around her waist, stopping her midair. Jessica thrashed wildly in Remmy's arms, but he held on.

"Don't Jessica," Remmy pleaded. "Show them that you're better than they are! Do what's right!"

"What's right?" Jessica snapped. "I'm doing what my nature demands. That is what's right!" She beat her fists against Remmy.

Remmy let go of Jessica. She had been his friend, some small piece of her still was, but she was a Red and that meant there were different rules for her. And just as Jessica couldn't demand that Remmy become a Red, he couldn't ask her not to be one. Jessica simply was who she was. He let her go. She dropped to the ground and dashed towards Ortiz.

The soldier scuttled backwards in the mud a few feet and then remained still. He had failed in his mission. The price of such failure was death.

-51-

The mud was cold. It should have been warm or at least tepid with the amount of blood mixed in, but it was just cold. Xander lay still, unmoving. He had been so close, so close to going home. But that rotten Emo terrorist, one that his sister seemed to *love*, had thrown him to the ground, accidentally discharging his last shot. He had no more leverage, had lost his one bargaining chip. It was over. It was time give up. What would Xander do now? He pushed his fingers through the mud, as if grasping for an answer. Suddenly, it was there.

Something heavy brushed against the tips of Xander's fingers. At first, he had thought that it was nothing more than a rock, but no rock was shaped like this. His fingers closed around the grip of Captain Ortiz's pistol.

Cora ran towards Remmy, his arms wrapped around Jessica's waist. The Red had shown some mercy on Remmy, perhaps remembering something from when they were once childhood friends, but Cora guessed that those memories would go only so far. As Cora paused by Xander, who was face down in the mud, Remmy put Jessica down, as if realizing that he couldn't really stop her from being what she was. Some piece of Cora screamed for her to stomp Xander into the ground for threatening to kill Remmy. Xander was her brother, but that seemed to matter little to him, so why should Cora value their blood bond? She took a deep breath, releasing the anger and walked past Xander.

Jessica crept toward Ortiz, a hungry, feline smile stretched across her face.

The gunshot cracked and split the air, shocking everyone, even Jessica. It wasn't the fact that it was a gunshot. No, there were plenty of those surrounding them. It was the fact that it so close, almost right behind them.

Xander stalked forward, gun held straight out in front of him. His face was streaked with mud, but his eyes glared from behind with an intensity Cora had only ever witnessed in her father.

"Don't move," Xander spat through gnashed teeth. He swept the gun back and forth.

Cora wished that she had retrieved her wrist gun from the ground. The decision whether or not to kill Xander suddenly seemed much clearer.

"Xander!" Samuel's voice boomed. "Stop this immediately." He spoke with a tone reserved only for indignant grandparents, a tone that superseded even that of mothers and fathers.

Xander spun to face Samuel.

"You're first," he said coldly and squeezed the trigger.

-52-

Samuel didn't want to hurt Xander. The boy was confused, disabled emotionally by his Em-Pak, and Samuel couldn't help but feel the responsibility of that resting upon his shoulders. But Samuel was also a pragmatist and Xander was a danger to Cora and Remmy. They had a right to live, to be free, and to be together. Xander couldn't be allowed to rob them of that. Samuel would do what was needed to keep his granddaughter safe. More so, he would do what was needed to give her the chance to live the life she had only just begun to enjoy.

It was too late for Xander he had made his choice, but Samuel had a choice to make as well. He had lived a long life, granted one riddled with mistakes and regret, but his mistakes were made in an honest attempt to do what was right. That counted for something, gave his life some meaning. Cora and Remmy deserved the same chance. Samuel remained fixed in place, his eyes locked with Xander's. The boy fully intended to pull the trigger, even if it was his grandfather on the other side of the barrel.

The gunshot *cracked* the ferocity of a small thunderclap. Even Xander appeared slightly surprised by the deafening roar. Captain Ortiz's muscled, trained arms easily controlled the pistol, handling the considerable and powerful kick of each discharged round. But Xander was young, had no experience with firearms and didn't anticipate the force of the gunpowder combusting within the small chamber. The pistol bucked back, slamming into Xander's face and splitting his lips. Blood gushed from the ragged zigzag that cut across his lips.

Samuel cried out in pain, spun in a half circle by the force of the bullet and collapsed to the ground. Cora rushed forward, but Xander twisted around, thrusting the gun into his sister's face.

"Next?" Xander grinned, intentionally popping the *T* at the end of the word and speckling Cora's face with his blood. He kept smiling, his teeth stained bright red and his Em-Pak chirping wildly. Xander moved cautiously around Cora and Remmy, keeping the gun trained on them. He made his way over to Captain Ortiz, who still sat on the ground stunned and bleeding. Jessica stopped when she heard the gunshot, but her muscles rippled with the desire to tear Xander apart. Her fingers clenched and unclenched as if in preparation for the violence she was about to visit upon Xander.

"Please," Xander scoffed looking at Jessica. "You may be some sort of infected, wild psychopath, but none of that means anything to a bullet. I just shot my own grandfather. Do you really think I'll hesitate to kill a piece of trash like you?"

Jessica laughed. "Bullets run out. Our numbers won't. At least not before your bullets do." She motioned over Xander's shoulder.

Xander turned to see a large group of Reds working around the sides of him, slowly closing in.

Jessica laughed again. "The only reason they haven't torn you apart is because I haven't given them permission to. You're mine to kill and all of this has gotten old. What I said before was true. I do miss my old life, sometimes, but I feel hungry *ALL* the time." Jessica stood up to full height. She was only slightly taller than Cora, but her presence emanated a threat, an unseen shadow that towered over her and promised violence well beyond her size.

Jessica held the severed piece of Captain Ortiz's arm in her hand. She laughed a good deep laugh, tore a chunk of flesh from the bone and tossed the rest of the meat to a nearby group of Reds. They fell on the limb in a feeding frenzy, devouring flesh and bone alike. The other Reds, as if spurred on by Jessica's offering loped forward, row upon row of pointed teeth bared.

"Remmy?" Cora asked.

"Get Samuel," Remmy said out the side of his mouth. "Go slow, okay? No sudden movements." Remmy knew or at least hoped that Jessica wouldn't hurt him or Cora, but the other Reds were a completely different story. They were hungry, enraged and smelled blood. Instinct and infection were calling the shots.

Cora backed towards Samuel, desperately searching the ground for her wrist gun, but it was lost in the thick mud. Samuel groaned loudly and rolled over. He was still alive, but his blood was doing little to calm the Reds. They appeared to have less self-control, or perhaps the desire to exert it.

The Reds slavered for meat, their jaws yawning and flexing. Long strings of saliva trailed from their mouths. Only Jessica appeared to have any semblance of control, which appeared to be quickly fading.

"Any time now, Captain," Xander snapped impatiently. "Any time you decide to be a soldier again would be convenient."

Ortiz fumbled with a small pocket on the shoulder of his uniform. Xander grew more and more impatient with Ortiz's clumsy movements and wasted time. The man was a soldier and blood loss or not, he needed to start acting like one.

"Ortiz!" Xander shouted. "Get your head in this. Right now! Soldier up, damn it! Right now, Captain Ortiz, or so help me, I'll shoot you myself!"

Ortiz shook his head like a dog emerging from the water and pulled a small silver packet from his shoulder pocket. He tore it open with his teeth and spat the ragged strip aside before pouring the contents of the packet over the stump at the end of his other arm. The caustic hiss of chemicals and smell of burning flesh filled the air. He winced, but fought through the pain. Ortiz examined the wound, content that it was cauterized and no longer bleeding. He climbed to his feet.

"My apologies," Ortiz said weakly. Touching the transmit button, Ortiz spoke into his helmet's radio. The pain he felt was pushed down, ignored. Ortiz, the man would have time for pain later, but Ortiz, the soldier had no such luxury. "This is Captain Ortiz calling the pilots of ERC gunships D6, H12 and J3. We are going scorched earth. Load all friendly Em-Pak signatures, including Xander Eldritch, into your targeting systems. All other heat signatures are fair game. Good hunting, gentlemen."

The three ERC helicopters swung back to the edges of the Reds' clearing, hovering like black clouds. *Whoosh, whoosh, whoosh.* The helicopters began releasing small missiles, targeting the areas where no friendly Em-Pak signals were shown.

The Reds frantically scattered, trying in vain to avoid the explosions. Remmy watched, his heart aching, as a small Red girl, perhaps only five or six, vanished in a pillar of greasy fire.

"Jessica, get them out of here!" Remmy yelled.

"Reds don't run," Jessica growled.

"You're their leader now!" Remmy argued. "Now lead them! They are going to die! Get them out of here!"

"But…" Jessica protested.

"Now!" Remmy screamed as he ran to help Cora pull Samuel up from the ground.

Jessica nodded and sprinted towards the woods and the safety of the trees. The other Reds pulled back and melted into the trees.

Cora pulled Samuel's arm around her shoulder as Remmy steadied his back. They needed to get to the woods. With the Reds gone, they were easy targets for the ERC soldiers.

Pain blossomed at the base of Remmy's neck, his stomach flip-flopped and threatened to empty its contents as stars and black spots exploded in his field of vision. On all fours, Remmy fought the urge to vomit and lost.

Xander stood over Remmy. The pistol he smashed into the back of Remmy's head was now trained on his sister and grandfather. Blood covered Xander's mouth and chin. A malevolent grin was carved into his young face.

"Go," Xander motioned with the gun. "You two serve no purpose, not any more. You're just embarrassments. I'm leaving you for the Reds to finish off. But Remmy? Remmy still has a purpose to serve, even if it's just to help me cause you pain. I'm taking him, Cora…or killing him. Either one works for me. You deicide."

"Xander," Cora growled. Xander was no longer her brother, maybe he never was. Xander held no affection for his sister. He was only her brother through blood and nothing more. He was a monster. He *is* a monster Cora corrected herself. A monster created by her father and fashioned in his image. Xander was everything that her father had wanted Cora to be and nothing that she wanted for herself.

"Save you idle threats, *sister*," Xander used the word mockingly. "You really thought you could keep me prisoner in some terrorist camp and there would be no recourse? You are seriously stupid, Cora, even more than I had given you credit for. This is the price for betraying your family."

"You're not my family!" Cora yelled. Xander laughed.

"Leave," Remmy coughed, long strings of vomit and drool hanging from his mouth. "Get Samuel out of here, Cora!" Xander once again wrapped his arm around Remmy's neck and yanked him up from the ground. The barrel of the gun remained focused on Cora and Samuel.

"But Remmy," Cora pleaded, "I just got you back. I can't lose you again, not after all of this."

"You won't," Remmy said. "Please, Cora, if there's any hope of fixing this, you need to get Samuel out of here now." As if to reinforce Remmy's point, the explosions began getting closer, picking off a handful of errant Reds that still remained, feasting upon the fallen ERC soldiers.

Tears streamed down Cora's face, but were quickly lost to the heat of the fires that raged on all sides of her. She pulled Samuel, semi-conscious, towards the woods. Her grandfather's steps were clumsy, but he had only been shot in the shoulder. He would be okay. Cora doubted that she ever would. Why would she come so close to saving Remmy only to have him snatched away from her by her own brother?

On the edge of the woods, Cora turned back towards the clearing. Only ERC soldiers moved, the Reds either dead or gone. One of the helicopters touched down and Cora watched as Captain Ortiz helped Xander into the cabin. Remmy, his hands bound together behind his back, was loaded in next. Ortiz finally climbed in and the helicopter lifted off the ground, tilted towards the Stele and disappeared over the horizon.

The clearing was silent, save for the crackle of a few fires. The only noise that could be heard was the pained sobs of Cora.

In that moment, Cora realized that a heart was little more than muscle and blood. It was an organ that lacked true purpose, functioning with no thought, only automatic impulse. That is, until it found a reason to beat. Her reason was gone, a black dot on the horizon that shrank with each passing second. Remmy was gone. There was no saving him this time.

-53-

Assemblyman Eldritch clicked off his video monitor. All and all, the day had been a good one. He had successfully shown the citizens that his control was absolute. Not only that, but he had retrieved Xander. Cora would have been ideal, having already been made known to the public and prepared, but did it really matter at this point? Eldritch could name a rabid chimpanzee as his successor and the citizens would go along with it. Xander would be acceptable. The boy had shown some real potential, real promise. Perhaps Eldritch had wrongfully assumed Cora was the best choice of successor.

"Report, Captain Ortiz," Eldritch barked into his radio.

"In transit back to the Stele, sir," Ortiz yelled over the deafening hum of the helicopter's rotors. "Unfortunately, sir, we were unable to recover your daughter or father, Mr. Eldritch."

"Yes," Eldritch snapped, "that was...regrettable, but I guess no more concern should be given to those two traitors. The Reds will finish what you couldn't."

"Yes, sir," Ortiz answered. "I concur, regrettable, but not a total loss, other than my arm of course."

"Put Xander on the radio, Captain," Eldritch demanded, ignoring Captain Ortiz's words and injury alike.

"Yes sir," Ortiz handed the headset to Xander.

"Father?" Xander answered.

"Yes, Xander," Eldritch said, his voice slightly softer than it had been for Ortiz. "How are you, son?"

"Much better now, Father," Xander responded. "Cora is such a disappointment. She removed her Em-Pak. She's an Emo, a terrorist."

"I know, Xander, but let's not focus on those things," Eldritch cut in. "We need to focus on the future, on your future."

An odd feeling bloomed in Xander's chest. It felt warm and hopeful – pride. As soon as the feeling arose, it was gone, another casualty of Xander's Em-Pak. Nonetheless, Xander's mind raced. Father was planning his future now, not Cora's. This was how it should have been from the beginning. Xander was always the better choice.

"I took an Emo prisoner," Xander added.

"Yes, I saw that, Xander," Eldritch responded. "We'll put him into a work camp or something of that nature as soon as we can. Eventually, he'll turn and have to be sanitized, but until then, he can dig holes or sort garbage."

"There may be a better use of him, Father," Xander said.

"And what might that be?" Eldritch asked.

"Father, he has knowledge of the Emos and the Reds. There is much to be learned from this Emo," Xander answered.

"I'm sure there is, Xander, but he won't talk. They never do," Eldritch said dismissively. "Once someone removes their Em-Pak, it makes them noncompliant, somewhat obstinate and petulant. We have tried numerous interrogation techniques and they are all *dead ends*." Xander and his father might have laughed at the morbid joke, if their Em-Paks hadn't been implanted, but since they were, the words were meant as nothing more than words.

"That's the best part, Father," Xander said, his voice rising slightly. "This one has never been implanted with an Em-Pak." The words hung between the two.

"Xander?" Eldritch said.

"Yes?" Xander answered, unsure of what to expect in response from his father.

"You have made me proud, son," Eldritch continued. "Very proud, indeed, Xander."

The odd feeling surged once again in Xander, though this time even slightly stronger. Then it was gone.

-54-

The woods were quiet, except for the footsteps of Cora and Samuel. He had regained some of this strength and now walked unassisted.

"I'm sorry, Cora," Samuel muttered. He had failed so many people with the creation of the Em-Pak, but failing Cora hurt the most, cut him the deepest. His granddaughter had seen a future beyond anything she had ever dreamt possible and now it was gone.

"It's not your fault," Cora answered. It was Xander's fault. It was her father's fault, but it wasn't Samuel's. He had tried to help, and been willing to trade his life to try to save Remmy. Cora would never have any feelings towards Samuel beyond admiration and love. Samuel was everything that a family member should be. He was everything that her father and Xander weren't.

"But it doesn't matter anyway," Cora sighed. "Remmy is gone. It's over." Cora had experienced many emotions since her Em-Pak was removed and most were intoxicating and enjoyable. These were not. Cora felt as if she were rotting from the inside, as if she might hollow out and collapse inward. How could people survive feelings like these? How could someone feel so hopeless and yet still wake up to face another day? Cora began to wish that she had been taken with Remmy or maybe that she had never made it out of the Red camp. Anything had to feel better than this, even death.

"No, Cora, it still matters. What you feel for Remmy will always matter," Samuel said. He was wrong to focus on his failures, his feelings of guilt. He had lived long enough to know that no emotion lasted forever and that nothing was forever. Cora had only recently had her Em-Pak removed. She had limited experience with emotions, especially the kind that now besieged her. "Cora, I know it feels hopeless right now, but it's not over. It's never over, unless you decide that it is. What you're feeling right now will pass. There will be better days and happy memories."

"Samuel?" Cora asked, her eyes red and watery.

"Yes?" Samuel answered.

"I love you, but please shut up," Cora said. She had never told her grandfather that she loved him, but she did, now more than ever. It made things feel slightly less hopeless to tell Samuel that she loved him, and to acknowledge that she was still capable of feeling something other than hopeless and to know that the feeling was returned. She still had people to love. She still could be loved. As long as she focused on that, Remmy wasn't truly gone. Cora's ability to feel love was rooted in Remmy. Had she never met him, she would have never known what love felt like, would have never been able to love others. As long as Cora held onto hope, held onto love, Remmy was never truly gone, but she still wanted him back.

"I never really liked those stiff upper lip speeches either," Samuel grinned. "Must be a family trait. But seriously, Cora, what you're feeling now has a place. Remember it. Remember how bad it felt and then become determined not to feel that way anymore. If you hold onto those feelings, they will drag you down to depths where they are the only thing you have left."

"I know," Cora sighed, "but what about Remmy? What did he mean that if there was any hope that we had to get you out of there?"

"I'm not completely sure," Samuel admitted, "but I think it has something to do with the Em-Paks."

"Em-Paks?" Cora asked. "Why would Remmy care about Em-Paks?"

"He doesn't," Samuel answered. "He cares about the people they are attached to. Remmy often talked to me about disabling the Em-Paks and thereby taking away the ERC's control over citizens. I think Remmy wants us to find a way to do that."

"Can't you just do that through the satellites or your computer or something?" Cora questioned.

"No, I've tried those routes, many times," Samuel answered. "The ERC has updated the system since I built it. More specifically, I think your father has. Those methods are blocked."

"But what about Remmy?" Cora demanded. The idea of disabling Em-Paks was a good one, but paled in comparison to any idea that resulted in the return of Remmy.

"Yes, well I think those two things may be connected," Samuel smiled.

"Connected?" Cora asked.

"If we are going to disable the Em-Paks and I can't do it remotely, then I have to do it directly," Samuel said.

"Directly?" Cora almost whispered. "Like at the main server in the Stele?"

"Yes," Samuel nodded. "I think that might be the only way to shut down the Em-Paks completely."

"Won't that leave people open to infection?" Cora asked. "A lot of people will die if you turn their Em-Paks off." She wanted Remmy back, more than anything. She wanted to have Remmy beside her again, but could she trade all those lives for his? Could she ask Samuel to do that when he already felt so much guilt?

"It could happen," Samuel continued, "but it might not. You, Remmy, and even Jessica have given me hope. Perhaps we should have never tried to control nature in the first place. Taking responsibility for our actions and emotions may have always been the best course, albeit, the most difficult for people to accept. Maybe some people are simply destined to be Reds and some aren't? I think it's time that we let citizens decide for themselves. Wouldn't you agree?"

"Yes," Cora answered. It was true that disabling the Em-Paks would result in infection for some, but not for everyone. Cora had survived it, so it stood to reason that others would as well. Then there were all of the other Emos, too. They lived every day without the ERC or an Em-Pak. People needed to be free to decide.

"So if we're going to the Stele anyway, we might as well find Remmy too," Samuel said as if he were suggesting a vacation detour. As if he and Cora might just stop off in the Stele and simply pick Remmy up.

"Samuel, you're basically talking about a revolution. We're going to need the other Emos to pull this off and even that might not be enough. It's definitely not going to be easy," Cora added, but her mind was already made up.

"Nothing worthwhile ever is," Samuel shrugged.

-55-

What had once been a large man was now a tangled bloody heap at Jessica's feet. His teeth were shattered and strewn across the ground. The few that remained whole had been torn out and cast aside in the dirt. Jessica looked wild, covered nearly from head to toe in blood. Her shoulders heaved with labored breaths as she glared at the circle of Reds surrounding her. Moments before, she sprang onto the man's back, ripping into him with tooth and nail. Her pointed teeth and powerful jaws had separated limbs, disassembling his body. Jessica needed to make sure her point was made and that there were no questions about her abilities. She was daring anyone to challenge her again. Killing Hatch had given Jessica her new role as leader of the Reds, but the four challengers she had torn apart after had solidified it. No one stepped forward.

"Are we done then?" Jessica growled. "Anyone else want to challenge my position?" Her fingers curled like claws and her teeth, slick with blood, shone like polished obsidian in the moonlight. There was no question who was in charge.

"Good," Jessica snapped. "Now we can get back to more important things. The ERC has drawn a line in the sand. They attacked us, killed countless Reds, but every day more join us. Reds are traveling from all over to unite. Our numbers are already larger than what they were before."

"But what's it matter? What are we going to do?" someone shouted from the safety and ambiguity of the shadows.

Jessica glared at the countless Reds gathered around her. Had she been able to see who shouted the question, she would have torn out their throat with her teeth.

"What are we going to do?" Jessica smiled. "The ERC made that decision for us. We're going to war!"

The Reds cheered, baring toothy maws and raising weapons. Remmy told Jessica to lead her people. She would lead them into battle with the ERC.

-56-

Remmy struggled against the thick leather straps that held him to the polished steel gurney. Men in masks and matching gray uniforms buzzed around him like a swarm of angry bees. Each had a different surgical instrument, but those were not what held Remmy's attention.

On a stainless steel tray sat a small box. A row of three jointed hooks extended from each side like the delicate legs of an insect. Thin, hollow wires spiraled around each hook. The device looked like an overturned dead spider, its legs curled inward. These small hooks would be embedded into Remmy's flesh, holding the device securely to the base of his neck. A large, delicate needle jutted from the center of the device. It was hollow and sharp. The implantation would be painful, the center needle lancing into the thick discs between Remmy's vertebrae. This was what would deliver the chemicals into Remmy's spine. Chemicals that would be traitorously replenished by his body, ensuring a constant supply for his Em-Pak. Chemicals that would travel to his brain and control his emotions.

The ERC doctors had explained all steps in this procedure to Remmy, but he found no comfort in this knowledge. Remmy thrashed on the gurney as the doctors tightened large straps across his chest, waist and legs. The gurney tipped forward, flipping upside down. Remmy hung from the bottom, only his shaved neck visible through the small opening in the base of the table.

Xander and his father watched from the theater seats perched high above the surgical floor. They wanted to be sure, to have first-hand knowledge that this Em-Pak implantation was successful. There were plans for Remmy and this was the first step. Remmy would be very important to Assemblyman Eldritch, very important to the ERC.

"Xander!" Remmy screamed, his body rigid with anger. "Xander, I saved you! I saved you, damn it!"

"And now I'm saving you," Xander whispered as he watched the doctors begin.

-57-

Though Assemblyman Eldritch had no idea, he had succeeded in far more than gaining control of the ERC. His grab for power was built upon false reports of Emos and Reds working together, something completely fabricated and created within his own imagination. Something his actions had now turned into a reality.

Miles away from the ERC and the Stele...
Something rustled in the bushes. Cora snapped around to face the sound, aiming her wrist gun in the direction of the sound.

"Easy there killer," Jessica teased as she stepped out of the undergrowth. The burns on the side of her face had healed in a twisted web of pink scars that made her appear even more dangerous and wild. The scarred flesh pulled one corner of her mouth up in a permanent half grin that exposed her vicious teeth.

Cora lowered her gun. If Jessica were there for a fight, or more specifically a meal, she wouldn't have made herself such an easy target. Cora never would have known she was there until it was too late. But Jessica wasn't here for either of those reasons.

"Sorry," Cora said, "things have been a bit tense around here lately."

"At least you don't have to worry about the Reds," Jessica shrugged. Her words were true. Since the battle with the ERC, the Emos had moved their camp deeper into the woods. No Red attacks had occurred since.

"I'm guessing we have you to thank for that?" Cora asked. "But why are you helping us? I don't get it."

"I'm not helping you," Jessica said. "I'm helping my people. It just so happens that you get some small benefit from me doing so."

"Enemy of my enemy, right?" Cora responded, though she suspected that Jessica's motivations went deeper than a simple hatred of the ERC.

"Yeah, something like that," Jessica nodded and changed the subject. "I've moved our hunting grounds closer to the cities." Her eyes gleamed with joyful memories of recent hunts. "Gives us a chance to prey on the ERC and everyone that stands with them. They hardly leave the cities anymore."

"That's good," Cora nodded. "We keep them contained, take away the citizens' ability to move around freely and things will get tense inside those walls. That will make the next part a little easier."

"Yup," Jessica agreed, "and it's just fun."

The two had formed an uneasy bond based upon mutual love for Remmy. Jessica remembered him as her childhood friend, still had some small shard of fondness for him. Those feelings combined with her desire to exact revenge on the ERC had solidified Jessica's side in the war. Cora's feelings for Remmy, though deeper and more complex than Jessica's, still spurred her to action. Both would lead their sides against the ERC. Both wanted Remmy free.

"Thank you," Cora blurted out, not knowing what to say next and finding the momentary silence uncomfortable.

"For what?" Jessica asked.

"Back there in the Red camp, you kept Remmy safe, at least as safe as you could," Cora answered. "You kept him who he was. Thank you."

"Wasn't me," Jessica shrugged. She began to walk away, but stopped and looked over her shoulder. "It was you. I can see that now. Could see it the minute he looked at you."

"Me?" Cora questioned.

"You're why he didn't get infected in the arena," Jessica nodded. "He really loves you, Cora. That kept him alive, kept him who he was. I hope it still does."

Cora blushed. It was strange, almost surreal to be discussing her feelings for Remmy with Jessica. She was a Red, supposed to be a monster and in many ways was, but nothing was as clear-cut as the ERC had said. Nothing was as black and white as Cora had once believed. Everything that Cora had been taught was wrong. With the passage of such a small amount of time, the world had been completely stood on its head.

"Yeah," Cora whispered, "I hope so too."

Jessica had already disappeared into the dense woods.

Acknowledgements

As always, the support from Gary and the rest of Severed Press is much appreciated.

The support of my friends and family has made not only this possible, but all things. I am indebted to each and every one of you.

The writers, bloggers and readers I have met along the way, whether you shared a review, some advice or just a joke, it was greatly appreciated.

Finally, to you the reader, thank you! Please feel free to find me on Facebook or Twitter.

5/14

Made in the USA
Lexington, KY
07 May 2014